DEJA

G000147121

For E.G and Mr C, with love

And in loving memory of Mumsie and my brother Stu

CHAPTER 1

"Abuse is never deserved; it is an exploitation of innocence and physical disadvantage, which is perceived as an opportunity by the abuser." Lorraine Nilon,

It is incumbent among the civilised not to commit a sexual crime such as incest. However, unfortunately there is a beast hidden within some men, a demon which is rare (but not unheard of) in women. There are certain monstrous indignities, cruelties and crimes that should not befall a human being, male or female, child or adult. High on the list, arguably just below murder, are rape and carnal abuse. I say "arguably" beneath murder because homicide is terminal to this life. Memories of such may remain in the next realm but that kingdom is a utopia of such serenity that it is swamped by forgiveness and peace of mind. There is no such barrier in the here-and-now of this world we all inhabit; such acts of violence and cruelty injure our enjoyment of existence, a wound which scabs and scars the memories of the afflicted making their life unhappy, unsociable and solitary because their trust in fellow human beings has been maliciously betrayed. You may think that the brainless thug who beats an old woman to the ground for her purse of pennies is a demonic beast. Quite right too; but so often in the case of sexual abuse the beast can hide behind decorum, civility and slick charm, a smart suited and booted man not the tattooed crew-cut yob you'd imagine. And only too often in the family circle these crimes of a forced, incestuous relationship remain unreported in a tongue-tied misjudgement by the victim to protect the culprit from a scandal that may afflict and sully the reputations of other nearest and dearest within the kinship. So why would a middle-aged man want to sexually abuse a small boy, especially if that child were his own son. I can only surmise; perhaps the father considered his son a threat to the affection and duty of his wife? Or maybe the child was a risk to the dominance of his kingdom? I don't know the answer and neither did a young child named Richard Pope whose autocratic father to diminutive son explanation was this:

'You see young Dicky; I own your mother and she gave birth to you. So, you also belong to me and are my right until you grow up.'

Richard thoughts were this about his father's one-sided and bias statement - No I'm not yours; I belong to me! But I can't stop you as I'm only six years old. And Richard now realised that his father's groping hands were inappropriate and unwanted, that the places of his body he touched were called "private parts" for a very good reason. But a small, unwilling-to-take-part and reluctant child is unable to prevent this deviant and dreaded incursion of his body from a powerful man who professed that he only did so because of his love for his son and that it was top-secret and a special affection he was not to tell Mummy about; it was a secret between just them. But Richard realised that this was rubbish and his father's actions were wrong; he knew this but was silenced by a ransom blackmail of sweets and fast, exciting trips in his father's E-Type Jaguar. However, over and above this he was frightened of what his father's reaction would be if he told someone what was going on, like the woman who suffers her partner's violence but remains silent to those who could help, a misguided loyalty navigated nervously by dread of the repercussions and consequences at a time when love and loathing are awkwardly confused. And also, there are the muddled elements of shame and shyness, tethered by the rubbery ropes of self-conscience that bungee between revenge and forgiveness, like the cruelly beaten dog that trots obediently alongside its' master yet dreams of mauling him. And the ghosts of abuse haunt the mind incessantly, bully decisions with self-reproach, turning the victim's persona to one of distrust and doubting to those who want to share his or her heart, except for those who are already and steadfastly etched within.

Richard's earliest memory was the retreat sanctuary from his father's abuse he found in the back garden of his parent's suburban London home. The year was 1993 and he was just five years old. Then and there he played with a brood of gnawing puppies, sunk from view within a forest of waterside grasses and reeds which danced around him in the gentle breeze and swamped his tiny yet parent-polluted virtue. He was dug deep and invisible in a fizzing efflorescence of pollen, darting insects and springing grasshoppers. The sun shone strongly from a cloudless, heat-belching sky and the reeds and grasses flung shadows over his soft skin and silken blonde hair, tattooing him in shadows like a tiger's pelt. And those beautiful, innocent, mahogany-brown eyes squeezed closed intermittently as his little nose hiccupped with sneezes in the pollen agitated air. It was on this day and during this momentary serenity that little Richard made a momentous decision. His father was a bad man; God was good as was Mr Kendal, the kind old gentleman who told stories about God's son, Jesus, at his Sunday school. Good was better than bad, warm compared to cold. It was harder to be polite and well-behaved than to be naughty, and being a little monkey could be fun. So the small lad decided, there and then, that he wanted to be like the man he saw every Sunday, to be good and un-mischievous and not wrong and horrid like his Daddy. Therefore, he must pay a childhood penance by sacrificing any elements of defiance and be forgiving to his father, like a goodly God-fearing woman who forgives her rapist by visiting him in gaol. This helps no one as the woman feels the cold agony of terror when she looks into those demonesque eyes; and the rapist enjoys what he sees, her vulnerable beauty which maliciously agitates his memory and excites his realisation that he must commit the crime again once he leaves internment.

But after a couple of years, young Richard became more resistant to his father's inappropriate approaches and had threatened to tell his mother about the abuse. Defiance was good in one way because it stopped his father in his tracks, but bad in another because he was packed away to the harsh, totalitarian confines of a boarding school where, at the tender age of eight, he became subjected to further acts of violence; the punches from bullies and the patronising bellows from the teaching and ancillary staff; even the fat cooks could be mean and intolerant. And Matron, that woman who paraded the dormitory area like a Nazi, could often be the worst of them all with big hands shaped especially for spanking.

Because of the tornado of thoughts slapping his mind in this alien, harsh environment – a vacuum from his mother's love, poor Richard couldn't sleep, his mind swirling with hard punches, demeaning shouts and his father's unwelcome gropes, all whacking his innocent judgement like a violent banshee. So, Richard was constantly tired and, consequently, fell behind with his schoolwork, a vicious circle that attracted more of his teacher's intolerance and deafening shouts. And so, he needed some method to induce sleep so as to catch-up with his classmates and please the teachers with his rejuvenated effort. Now young Richard knew how to do this because he'd once overheard a heated conversation between his parents.

His mother had asked her husband accusingly, 'Why do you drink so much whisky when you come home from work?'

To which his father had shouted this reply (and it wasn't normally a shouty household as his mother avoided her husband), 'Because it helps me sleep.' That comment had roosted in the boy's memory.

Now Richard's housemaster was a ginger-bearded Scotsman called Mr Brodie, and Brodie kept bottles of whisky on a shelf in his study. To young Richard these bottles looked the same as those he'd seen his father use to decant that golden liquid into a glass, and there were so many clumped together on that shelf that the housemaster couldn't notice one disappearing now and again. The problem, of course, was the danger of getting caught. On the up side, Brodie's study was never locked as none of the pupils would dare trespass within for fear of incurring his wrath. On the down side the burglary would have to occur at night when all the school was sound asleep, a spooky time for a young lad with a vivid imagination and who'd rather be wrapped within a warm cocoon of cotton sheets and woollen blankets. Nonetheless, the medicine for sleep was urgently needed and so, on the night following his masterly idea, he embarked upon the theft, adopting the brave persona of his invisible friend, James (named after 007), tiptoeing all alone through spooky night shadows - you know where headless ghosts, Frankenstein and Dracula lurk in a child's imagination – down long, dark corridors that were teeth-chatteringly eerie to his frightened and naive innocence. But he acquired his target (appropriately labelled "Teachers") and then shuffled the others to hide the gap then returned to bed; the burglary was never discovered and neither were those undertaken in the future because he hid the bottles in a toilet cistern and decanted nightly doses into an empty shampoo bottle.

*

It was because of his uncaring upbringing and the abuse he'd suffered as a child that Richard decided upon his vocation early in life, that he would put right the wrongs of his past and enter the Ministry of the Anglican church (ironic really with the surname of Pope). So, he went from school to a residential Theological College in London, his faith in God and copious amounts of whisky having stretchered him through a troubled childhood and turbulent teens paving his way into manhood. And a fine man he'd evolved into, tall, dark-haired with benevolent, mahogany tinted eyes and with the handsome looks of a screen idol; an Adonis blessed with a sugary, soft-spoken and munificent kindness that attracted the ladies to his church in large numbers leaving little room for the men of the parish. But no one suspected his dependence on strong alcohol as his breath was always minty clean and fresh, disguised by mouth-wash. Of course, Richard was so devout (some may say sanctimonious) with his theologies and beliefs, that he hadn't taken a wife or girlfriend, preferring the celibacy ethos of the Roman Catholic faith which, without being selfish or self-centred, proved to him a certain devotion to the Almighty. Besides the women he had known in the past had always been unnecessarily concerned about his at-home drinking habits, some to the point of nagging; he could do without that!

There was one more foible to Richard's character and that was his love of his Triumph Speed Triple motorcycle, a weakness because motorcycles and whisky are not the best bedfellows and should be kept a deep gorge apart. Richard tried his best to adhere to the wise advice of his conscience, but it wasn't always possible especially if he'd had a skin full and overindulged the night before.

*

Urbanised people don't understand the delicacy of the countryside; rural folk are confused by hubbub of towns. Richard's Parish was remote, a small and quaint, hewn-stone village called New Milton (ironic because it was an ancient settlement and most of the houses were very old) tucked away in the county of Dorset and set idyllically within the shade of a leafy vale; a little haven of peacefulness where wealthy people from London retired to end their days; a sanctuary of forgiveness for the prurient sins they'd committed during their Beatle-mania youth. The following is painted with a hint of sarcasm - Of course these were not selfish people who'd sent property prices rocketing and consequently pushed the less-well-off locals out of the villages into the towns; no perish the thought and quite the opposite. Nor were they the type who'd been savagely selfish in their careers and ruthlessly worked themselves to the top of the ladder and who now wanted to salve their bruised consciences with the ointment of rural life; birds, bees, fluttering butterflies and sea-side strolls. And when they moved into New Milton most of them began to attend church, a wholesome and purposeful way of life they hadn't had time for before, but which would now atone for the ills of their past. Retirement was the time to expiate for a life-time of selfish greed and pave the way to Heaven's gates with the slabs of righteousness; being

7

so good and holy soothes the soul and erases wrong-doing with charitable clemency. The church with its' wise and goodly, God-fearing whispering walls and echoed prayers were the bleach to the toilet pan of sin, washing histories of wrongdoing downwards into the sewers and into the flames of Hades. After all, it makes perfect sense as the Bible and God are all about forgiveness. At least that is the sinner's hypocritical thinking, to leave their misspent past behind and follow in the footsteps of the virtuous.

"It is easier for a camel to pass through the eye of a needle than for a rich man to enter the kingdom of God." Mark 10:25

*

The year was 2012 and Richard was 24 years old and had almost completed his curacy as a Deacon in the Anglican Church (a Deacon is a Priest with "L" plates.) In some ways he was lucky, because his spiritual mentor, the Reverend Henry Clotworthy, was a worn-out, lazy man in his early 60's with a crescent spill of grey around his glistening bald-head, a bulbous stomach like a beach-ball and a lawn of frowzy stubble encrusting a baggy double-chin. Clotworthy was rarely seen by the parishioners (usually only at Holy Communion) and preferred to let young Richard undertake the day-to-day running of the church. After all, from the idle vicar's point of view, Richard was in training and the best way to learn is to do-so on your own, and put into practise that theological education taught at college prior to becoming a Curate. And Richard didn't mind, although a little help now and again would have been useful. And there was one more thing to put into the equation; the Reverend Henry Clotworthy was about to retire from the priesthood after over 30 years of loyal (if a little lackadaisical) service to New Milton and he would hand the divinely lustred reins of the church (blessed with a patina of prayers) over to Richard in a few weeks' time since Richard had completed a year as a Deacon and was due to be ordained as a Priest. At least that was the plan because no one could possibly foresee the ominous change of events that would befall poor Richard.

New Milton church was a grey-stone building with hewn golden-arched windows (some aflame with a mosaic of stained glass) and a square, buttressed tower with a pinnacle atop each corner, each one lancing the heavens like fingers pointing to God. It was approached by a long, gravel path which slew between lop-sided grave stones on which the epitaphs had been blurred by acid rain, ravaged by icy winds, caked with orange lichens and strangled by ivy. It was the kind of cemetery that conjured an awed respect and reverence into the mind, but one you wouldn't walk through alone at night. The church building itself - entered via a heavy, arched portcullis-like oak door with a rusted and well-worn hooped handle - stretched back to the early 12th century when the Normans ruled the British throne; a history those-in-the-know could identify by architectural features, especially a large, round, Romanesque carved arch where the nave (the bit in which the pews paraded in regimental style) abutted the chancel (where the altar is found). The rest of the stone-hewn, echo-whispering chilly caverns that formed the place of worship had been renovated, modernised and preserved by previous and ensuing generations and that stone tower had been added in the 15th century.

On this Sunday, a beautiful, daffodil emblazoned early spring one, the church was full, pews packed shoulder-to-shoulder with affluently dressed parishioners, women pushed to the front, to admire the wisdom of their handsome young curate, and a few men struggling for room at the back. Now Richard was blessed with that un-judgemental nature common to most members of the clergy, so ignored the sweet aroma of vanity and unholy avarice polluting the air and stirring the ambience by wafting up from the variety of perfumes that permeated the pews before him.

Bouncing sunlight, gilded and abloom like the daffodils outside, spun the atmosphere of the building in between elongated shadows, inspiring a jaunty satisfaction to settle in silence among the congregation as Richard ascended the pulpit to orate his sermon. It was close to Easter, the life after life egg of reincarnation, and so the subject of Jesus the Messiah was order of the day. Richard told his congregation in a voluptuously worded sermon all about the wonders of the Saviour Son of God and the many miracles he had performed; turning water to wine, feeding the five thousand, curing a blind-man's sight and more. His audience listened with a respectful silence, devout attentive faces most trying to restrain a yawn!

At the end of the service, Richard habitually stood inside the entrance porch and greeted members of the congregation as they left the building, all of them bidding the curate with a deferential handshake and pious smile before venturing homeward to a roast beef and Yorkshire pudding feast of gluttony.

When the church was empty, Richard went into the Vestry and found the store of communal wine; he glugged back a bottle (which he would replace) before dis-robing then locking up the church. After that he walked to his motorcycle (leaning lazily on its' side-stand) jumped onto the machine and headed for home (a little one-bedroom flat kindly rented for him by the diocese on instruction by the district Bishop). And it was a beautiful day for motorcycling, the foliage of birthing spring flicking past him in lime-green blurry caverns which rose above and around the speeding bike in vernal opulence, tunnelling the twisty and turning country lanes that snaked fearlessly ahead. Richard was exhilarated by the thunderous burble from the bike's exhaust and felt the speed-rush of wind flicking, pattering and pounding against his clothing. So, he twisted back the throttle further and the bike leapt ahead like a tiger pouncing at prey. But, with a mind fuzzy from communal wine, he'd forgotten how sharp the approaching corner was, forgotten until it was too late and he, and his prized machine, was sent scuttling into the trees. The machine was travelling around sixty miles per hour when Richard jumped off, like a pilot ejecting from a stricken plane. Then he heard an ominous smash as the bike hit a tree trunk and Richard was sent into a somersault spin down a hill, a painful and bruising eddy, whipped by twigs and low branches, cannonballed through thorny shrubs and brambles, assaulted by mud and grasses in a spinning green vortex until unconsciousness relieved the swelling agony like water to the flame. No sensation now, just a muted and overwhelming blackness.

But unbeknown to Richard, who grasped the tenuous remnants of life with frail fingers (like stamping upon the digits of one who clung to the edge of a precipice), an observant passer-by (a Company Rep on his travels) had noticed the recently scarred vernal landscape and had stopped his car and got out to investigate. He found Richard's seemingly lifeless body smashed, in a grotesque and bloodied twist, against the mighty trunk of an oak tree. The motorist knew not to move the body or try to remove the helmet (as this could extinguish any remnant sparks of life) so he urgently dialled 999 on his mobile phone to call for an ambulance with that just-in-case and better-to-be-safe-than-sorry intent; no reception down here so he'd better climb back up to the road and try to phone from there.

But Richard's spirit had drifted away, not to that golden city where cherubs on clouds twang harps; his soul was headed elsewhere towards a stench and the grey, cloying atmosphere of death.

CHAPTER 2

ARBEIT MACHT FREI, WORK SETS YOU FREE

"The belief in a supernatural source of evil is not necessary; the human race alone is quite capable of every wickedness." Adapted from a quote by Joseph Conrad.

Richard's spirit had slipped back in time caused by a regressive portend known as pre-incarnation, in other words his drifting life-force had re-entered the person he was in a previous life, that moment before his errant soul was reincarnated sometime previous to his former self's death. To explain a little further, we've all experienced that odd sensation of déjà vu, that familiarity feeling that you've met someone before but know damn well you haven't; or been somewhere you clearly recognise despite the fact you've never been there before. Well, the only explanation for this phenomenon is that you have met this acquaintance or entered that room or scene before, albeit in a previous or future life. Unfortunately, we can't choose who we become on reincarnation after death. If we could we'd all be intellectual multi-millionaires making currencies worthless due to burgeoning inflation, thus causing an ensuing lust for greed that would ignite wars and scupper everyone's hopes and ambitions. Likewise, we cannot choose who we might have been in a previous life, in other words we cannot select the being or the gender of such for our pre-incarnation. For Richard this proved very unfortunate because his ethereal inner-being had slithered back to the late summer of 1944 to his former self, a beautiful, twenty-one-year-old blonde woman who just happened to be (allegedly – and I will address this later on) one of the cruellest women that ever set foot on this planet: SS-Rapportfuhrerin (senior female guard of the Schutzstaffel – Protection Squad) Irma Grese (pronounced Greasa [like pressure]); known as "The Hyena of Auschwitz" or "The Blonde Beast." Now Richard didn't realise he'd become Irma and, obviously since in 1944 he wasn't yet born, she knew nothing about him.

It was 6.30 in the morning and beautiful Irma (known as Iggy to friends and colleagues) was sat at her dressing table in her quarters at the Auschwitz Concentration Camp. She observed her lovely reflection in the mirror, an image radiated by the soft glow shimmering from a table-lamp which tinted her beauty with an osmosis of delicate shadows as she stroked a comb down her shoulder-length wavy hair; striking blue eyes with a lagoon of benevolence swimming in their sapphire depth, plump kiss-me lips between soft, pink cheeks; an overall gentle beauty that lured the lust most men. When she'd finished styling her hair, Irma commenced a necessary daily routine and splashed copious amount of Chanel perfume on her neck, wrists and under her nose in an attempt to counteract the stench of death and burnt flesh that soused every grain of soil and particle of dust within the vast camp complex. She'd noticed the terrible and disgusting odour on arrival at Auschwitz almost eighteen months earlier and recognised it by recalling the dreadful smell of a putrid, grub-captured carcass of a fox she'd once stumbled across as a child. But this gut-retching stink at the death camp was far, far worse; a foul odour of fatality and faeces stewed by the rank ammonia of festering urine; a nauseating and reeking stench her senses could not acclimatise with nor get used to and which resulted in her having to keep the bedroom windows sealed closed even in the fetid heat of a Polish summer. Not even the carrion fowl or buck-toothed rat could tolerate the smell around here and so, creature-wise, the camp was solely the domain of scuttling cockroaches, zipping flies and writhing maggots.

Irma then bent down and began to roll a stocking up her subtly muscled left leg; she felt the orgasmic thrill of self-satisfaction by stroking herself, slowly and erotically towards her groin; a sensual tingle of finger-tips caressing her thigh while slowly clipping the stocking-top to the suspender-belt. She then took a deep, gratified breath before reaching down to her right foot and rolling the other stocking upwards while experiencing the same erogenous and stimulating pleasures as before. It was as if the orgy of wine and sex with Doctor Josef Mengele ("The Angel of Death" who was still gurgling wicked dreams in her bed) the previous evening and night had not fulfilled her ravenous sexual appetite.

The infrequent grunts behind her stuttered to a barrage of snorts and SS-Hauptsturmfuhrer (Captain) Mengele sat up in bed, a deadly dawn of awakening. The Doctor was over ten years older than Irma but had the looks of a movie star, a man she thought resembled Cary Grant but with a quirky gap in his upper front teeth which she found strangely appealing.

'Why are you going to work so early, my beauty?' he asked to Irma's reflection in the dressing-table mirror.

'Because I'm on punishment from Commandant Baer at the moment,' she replied, copying Mengele's technique by eying his reflection in the looking glass.

Mengele chuckled. 'Oh, you naughty girl!' He grinned churlishly at her image. 'What did you do to earn Baer's displeasure?'

Irma pouched each of her plump, cushion-soft breasts into the cups of a bra then reached backwards with the straps to the indent of her spine and skilfully (practise makes perfect) located hook to eye. Then, while slipping her arms through the undergarment's shoulder straps, she said, 'I was caught not wearing my cap while on duty.'

'And what, may I ask, is your punishment?' he questioned

Irma unexpectedly spun on her stool and faced him. There was an angry disquiet alight in her blue eyes. 'I have to oversee a gang of Jewess whores who are building a stone road to transport dead bodies to the crematorium. The fucking Jews keep dropping dead like flies around here, so Baer ordered the new road's construction.'

Noticing the annoyance that flamed her eyes, the doctor replied carefully. 'I know; so many are shot for being disobedient and you have to be careful not to fall over their bodies. But I'm told it's worse in some of the other camps.'

Irma was now concentrating on buttoning-up the front of her open-neck blouse. 'I've only got a couple of days of punishment left to do,' she said as she glanced out of the window up at the sky, a view above the roofs of the red-brick SS guard barracks. 'At least it looks like it'll stay dry today,' she commented as she stood, crossed the room to her wardrobe, followed by the lascivious doctor's ebony eyes that studied the salacious wiggle of her panty-shrouded bottom. She then opened the wardrobe door and withdrew her uniform, a light-grey jacket, with a white War Merit Cross medal pinned to the left breast, and a knee-length skirt. Irma then slipped into the ensemble, zipped up the skirt, buttoned the jacket then strapped a holstered Lugar pistol around her waist. She then bent down and struggled into some knee high but femininely fashioned black boots, then completed the uniform by placing a black side-cap atop her head (slightly askew in a military fashion and sinisterly adorned by the death's head skull-and-bones emblem of the SS;) finally she picked up a riding-crop whip, which she'd adapted with a cellophane tip (for extra pain and cutting power to any prisoners unlucky enough to incur her displeasure,) and tucked it inside her belt. Irma was now immaculately smart as she wandered over to the Doctor, now propped up against the bedstead by a pillow, smoking a cigarette; she kissed him gently on the forehead then proceeded to leave the room.

She was followed out by Mengele's words, 'I'll see you later for the selection' (selection meaning choosing which prisoners were to be murdered in the gas chambers that day).

Irma closed the bedroom door behind her then strode purposefully along a corridor and down a single flight of stone steps to the bottom where she swung open the door to the dog kennels. Khan, her German shepherd, recognised her immediately and began a tail wagging frenzy from within his cage. Irma approached the animal; slid back the bolt on the cage-door and the excited-to-see-her animal sprang out and swirled around her in a joyous flurry of leaping paws and licking tongue.

'Calm down, Khan,' Irma demanded while she quickly tethered the dog with a leash she'd taken from a hanging hook behind the door. This seemed to sober the animal to obedient duty, a fierce and devout guardian-of-owner role he suddenly adopted with pricked-up eared sobriety.

The pair headed outside into the meaningless drabness of day-break and also that stifling stench which even caused the dog to sneeze offensively. As they wandered along within a red-brick, death-infused cavern of buildings, sweating with summer dew as if fevered by despondency, other SS guards (mostly men) were beginning their day whilst some were returning to their quarters after a night-shift. And all of them that crossed Irma's path eyed the young woman's beauty with envy-of-Mengele admiration and offered a polite tip of the cap greeting, some even a gusty salute. But Irma's demeanour was on the change, that Jekyll and Hyde trait of a young woman's personality, (one stewed by conflicting hormones) that changes with the wind; gone from her eyes were those blue lagoons of tolerance; she was becoming drunk on malignant intent with thoughts about the day that lay ahead, especially her charge Jewesses in the road building team. And it seemed as if Khan had similar ideas too as he stretched his leash and pulled impatiently ahead.

Irma was at times like a cultured rose, one that blooms proudly with sweet perfume; but she could also be the knotted briar that chokes with a scramble of sharp thorns.

Auschwitz was the largest of the Nazi concentration camps and was split into three main camps and three sub-camps. Irma was assigned to Birkenau 2 (Camp BIIC), the extermination camp where the gas chambers and crematoriums were located; she was the most senior female guard there(but not in the whole camp) and formed part of a large SS sentry assigned to guard between twenty and thirty thousand Hungarian Jewish women (the numbers varied from day to day, reduced by mass executions and added to by daily consignments of new prisoners from cattle-carriage trains) packed like tinned frankfurters (at least five women in each single wooden plank bunk and sometimes as many as twelve) into around thirty timber prison blocks originally used (before the German invasion of Poland) by the Polish army for horse stabling. Pinned to a structural post in the middle of each block was an ominous tin sign which read "Eine lause dein tode," which translated means "One louse means your death."

Irma and her dog strode steadfastly through the guarded gate into the female prisoner's compound enclosed entirely by a lethal barb-wire electric fence supported by gaunt concrete posts. These were about ten feet apart and high and bowed inwards at the top (to prevent scaling in a power-cut) and resembled hangman's gallows, an unfortunate omen to the young woman's unknown fate. She and the dog continued walking alongside the fence and behind the long sides of several oblong dormitory blocks until she reached the first of forty-six containing the Hungarian Jewesses. Irma entered the first of these and, engulfed by dark, sleeping shadows, lashed her whip against the wall to gain the inmates attention. Then, she shouted the names of twenty women and demanded them to speedily gather around her (a bunch of workers she'd previously selected for road duty because they were young, fit and understood German.) Once they had, she led them outside and asked a machine-gun-wielding, SS man (luring his compliance with a playful flutter of eyelids) if he wouldn't mind accompanying her and the troupe of women to their workplace which was close to the gas-chamber/crematorium location. And Khan had jumped to duty too; was on a strained leash and barking wildly at the group of women prisoners dressed in tattered rags*, jaws snapping violently in an angry, saliva-stringed display of menacing sharp fangs.

*Hungarian women did not wear the infamous striped suits nor were they tattooed with a number.

(Although the Nazis had initially tried to disguise the heinous purpose of the death camp from the inmates, the building of four huge crematoriums finished by early 1943 and their gushing, black bone-meal smoke gave the game away to all who witnessed it, although some remained sceptical to the murderous intent. By 1944 the camp was full to bursting point and the killing-programme had intensified to such a degree that most of those brought in on cattle-carriage trains were being sent straight to the gas chambers. All the inmates knew why they were imprisoned at Auschwitz, that the Nazis considered them as enemies-of-the-state and they were stuck inside these unescapable compounds to be eliminated; but those lucky enough to curry favour with their captors or be proactive hard-grafters within a work-party were usually kept safe from the daily fatal selection processes.

So, although it was shocking for the Hungarian women to know the purpose of the gas chambers and crematoriums, they simply turned a blind eye when they were forced to walk past them and inwardly prayed for the safety of themselves and their loved ones [if these loved ones were still alive]. But Irma tried to choose her moments to march them past the gas chambers so to avoid mutiny by offending the women's fragile sensibilities at witnessing a death-queue being marshalled inside with jabbing gun-barrels; only the most hard-hearted members of the SS could observe such a dreadfully cruel spectacle.)

But on this particular day there was no avoiding another ghastly sight, for outside one of the crematoria was a pile of at least one hundred dead bodies straggled together in a grotesque web of emaciated flesh and bones, bruise-blackened and as brittle as charcoal. Guarding them was a man she recognised, SS Haptscharfuhrer (Quartermaster Sergeant) Otto Moll, a man who was in charge of the crematoria and one with an avidly wicked reputation that matched his etched-on-face sneer, someone Irma despised for his excessive cruelty; for it was common knowledge that he had once thrown several children and babies alive into flaming pits, a stomach-turning act of brutality that even Irma considered was overstepping the mark.

Despite her misgivings about the man, Irma told her escort-guard to hold the group of women where they stood, then crossed the courtyard to speak to him. 'Why are all those bodies heaped up there?' she asked, gesturing at the grisly mound.

'Two of the crematoria have broken so I'm twenty-three ovens down at the moment,' Moll explained with a sinister twist accentuating that sneer on his malevolent face.

'But there'll be thousands more executions today including hundreds arriving by train,' said Grese. 'How will you cope?'

As Irma asked the Sergeant this question, two men in work-soiled blue and white striped suits scurried out of one crematorium around to the pile of bodies; they quickly selected one limp, flagging corpse from the top of the pile and, like scuttling beetles, carried it back into the building.

Moll answered her question. 'I've requested that the engineers come and fix the problem, so hopefully we'll be up and running later on.'

Irma turned away and looked back across the courtyard at the escort-guard; she shrugged and gave him a resigned look of exasperation. She then beckoned at him to lead the work-party women over and to follow her to the place where the road was being constructed. When they reached the site, Irma instructed all the women to pick up two heavy rocks (one in each hand) from inside a nearby abandoned wooden cart which slumped askew and bowing down with handles touching the ground as if knelt in lamentation. There was nothing unusual about this as the rocks were used to build the road. But on this day Irma Grese had other ideas. She had been upset by the sight of the heaped bodies outside the crematoria, not in a sad way because she was used to the practises at Auschwitz, but angrily because the slaughtering of Jews was delayed which would result in a dearth of bed spaces and blankets.

So, she turned to the female work-party and said sharply, 'Now ladies, before you start work today, you'll all need a little sport to warm up those muscles.'

She then ordered all the twenty women to kneel on the ground in a line and hoist the rocks above their heads and hold them there. Due to malnourishment and their consequent weakened condition, it only took a few seconds before their poor, thin arms started to tremble, wilting like spaghetti to the weight of the rocks.

Noticing this, Irma un-holstered her luger and pointed it threateningly at the women, swaying it along the line to ensure they continued to hold the rocks high.

Khan sensed the tension and began to bark fiercely at the women again, spitting saliva and stretching the leash to stand on his hind legs, restrained by Irma's struggling grasp.

'Hold them up!' Grese demanded irately, her eyes icy cold while she grappled to restrain the power of Khan. 'Only strong women can build roads. Weak women are useless and should be sent to the gas chambers.'

The women were terrified and teary-eyed, their pathetic, sullen faces twisted agonisingly to the weight of the rocks. Then one of them collapsed to the ground like a string-snapped puppet, limbs flailing in a tear-spluttering heap of exhaustion.

Irma holstered her pistol, walked over to the escort-guard and handed him Khan's leash to hold the dog. She said mildly to the other women in the line, 'You can put the rocks down now.' She then approached the fallen woman who was struggling in the dust, trying to scramble back up onto her knees. Brandishing her whip and slicing the air with whistling swishes, Irma struck the woman with it on the right side of her face, slicing it open and drawing blood; then the left cheek and another bloody wound. Finally, and with all the strength she could muster, she whipped her victim across the bosom; the woman's blouse bloomed red, blotting the spreading stain of blood. She then ordered her distraught and hysterically sobbing victim to stand up and return to barracks, adding coldly 'I will deal with you later.'

Doctor Mengele then entered the scene, puffing on a cigarette and nonchalantly uninterested in what was going on. He was smartly dressed in the grey uniform and cap of an SS Captain with shiny black boots which almost stretched to his knees. He looked so dapper, alluring and deliciously handsome to Irma's eyes. He smiled fondly at her then walked over to her and whispered into her ear (so the others couldn't hear), 'It's time for a selection parade.'

19

'Okay,' she replied excitedly. 'I'll just get my dog.'

So, she approached the escort-guard, took Khan from his hold and said to him, 'I won't be long, an hour or so.' She smiled at him in a deliberately sensual way to invoke his agreement with her next request, 'Would you mind keeping an eye on my workers?'

How could the guard refuse after the beautiful, twinkle-eyed suggestive look she'd just given him? And there might be a slim chance that his luck could be in with Irma one day! That thought aside, he couldn't deny Mengele, his superior, if the doctor chose to intervene; so, he smiled and nodded his agreement.

'Thank you,' she said. 'Make sure they work hard. You can see what they've done before.' She pointed at a section of finished road surface. 'Simply get the Jewish whores to chisel the rocks to shape then dig them into the ground and level them to one another and across the road. Don't worry, the bitches know what to do; you just make sure it's done properly and not slap-dash....Thanks again,' she added before turning away and re-joining Mengele. Then the pair strode away, side by side, Irma taut-leash-pulled by her excited dog.

Mengele, Grese and the dog trod the route Irma had taken the work-party along earlier. It was now a little after nine o'clock that morning and the sun was beginning to struggle upwards in the unsullied, azure sky. Irma realised it was going to become another scorching hot August day as they approached the vastly depleted pile of corpses (due to the pair of scurrying prisoner's labours) laying outside Moll's crematoria. She also realised that the simmering summer heat would greatly intensify the appalling smell if more corpses (those from today's selections) were dumped in the open due to malfunctioning ovens. She sighed deeply at the realisation and looked up; only two of the five chimneys were belching out black smoke.

While still walking alongside Mengele, and realising the broken ovens hadn't yet been repaired, Irma glanced at the doctor and said, 'Do you know that only half the crematoriums are working?'

Mengele glimpsed back at her. 'Yes, I popped my head in the door earlier and spoke to Sergeant Moll. It's the power supply to the exhaust fans that's broken and the engineers are in there now trying to fix it.' He put his hand on Irma's shoulder to stop her. 'Wait here a moment and I'll find out how much progress they've made.'

The Doctor was gone for at least ten minutes. When he returned, he said to Irma, 'Sorry I was so long I had to speak to Moll. Apparently, someone had sabotaged the electric supply and cut the main wire. As its mainly dead bodies enter the place, it must be someone who works in there.' He rubbed his chin thoughtfully. 'It wouldn't be any of us so it must be one of the Jewish Sonderkommandos* who work there. Anyway, I've asked Moll to replace all the prisoners that work in there because the existing staff will visit the gas chamber today.'

*Sonderkommandos were Jewish men and women selected for the jobs no one else wanted to do like clearing corpses out a gas chambers and working in the crematorium. Being a Sonderkommando was a death sentence in itself as they were regularly replaced with new.

"Birkenau simmered in the July sun like some hideous brew, a witch's potion of blood, sweat, smoke, and excrement worthy of something the weird sisters might have cooked up in Macbeth."

— J. Michael Dolan

"I'm the son of two Holocaust survivors. As a child I heard from one of my parents' best friends about living through Mengele's infamous selection process at Auschwitz. He haunted my nightmares." Ronen Bergman.

Doctor Josef Mengele possessed the menacing mind-set of a serial killer (albeit without actually getting his hands dirty) and so delighted in his duty at the selection process; Irma (having some particles of a woman's altruistic nature) was not so keen. Nevertheless, as a young girl, the ethos of Nazi ruthlessness had been indoctrinated into her when attending The League of German Girls (Hitler Youth for young women.) She had been taught that Jews were responsible for Germany's loss of the First World War and the subsequent economic failure that sunk the nation into the doldrums. In consequence this sematic race was the national enemy of the Germanic people. This misguided theory was further hammered home to Irma by the Maria Mandel School while training to become a Female Guard, conducted at the Ravensbruck Concentration Camp prior to her being posted to Auschwitz. It was at Ravensbruck that she first witnessed the cruelty of the process known as The Final Solution.

The Doctor stood in the warm sunshine outside the first of the forty-six dormitory blocks (the one in a long line of others and closest to the gas chambers) which contained the Hungarian Jewess' prisoners. He was waiting for Irma and four other guards to empty the building so that the selection process could begin. He didn't have to wait long before the women inmates started to spill out of the door like a swarm of agitated insects, and he gestured for them to head towards the electric fence. This was a procedure the women were quite used to as it happened every morning and evening, either for roll call or for selection to the gas chambers. Because of the number of Jews, and other ethnic undesirables, rolling into Birkenau from the cattle-carriage train transports (most of which were being sent straight to their death) there hadn't been enough room in the gas chambers for those in residence at the camp, so a selection process in the women's camp hadn't taken place for a few days much to Mengele's disappointment.

To avoid SS wrath and wicked abuse (and the very real threat of being shot dead), more than one thousand female inmates, old, middle-aged and young, quickly followed twice daily (sometimes more) procedures and assembled into four military-like lines in front of the fence, with just enough room for Mengele to walk in-between. The gathering stood obediently, still as marble statues as he moved over to the crowd, stood mid-way in front of them and positioned himself about twenty feet back from the front line; then Irma and her dog joined him and stood by his side.

Mengele then began to issue instructions adopting a smarmy tone quite akin to his character. 'Now Ladies, as it's such a lovely day I want everyone to strip off all their clothing.' This request irritated Irma in an envious and you-should-only-have-eyes-for-me way. So, she lasered a questioning glare up at him. He sensed her annoyance so bowed his head and whispered an explanation into her ear. 'I simply want to properly examine their physiques to see who's fit and strong enough to be set work duties and those who are frail and old who'll be sent to the gas-chambers.' He then looked back at the group of prisoners who were anxiously stripping themselves of clothing while being watched by leery-eyed, marauding guards with guns strapped to their shoulders. As soon as all the women were naked, the Doctor walked over to the first in the line and began his inspection, spitefully trampling over their clothing in a deliberate and despotic display of Nazi-to-Jew supremacy, finger outstretched and counting. He quickly came across a frail, hunched-up old woman 'Stand forward,' he growled at her. Next a young girl to whom he made the same demand. It took Mengele (followed by two guards also making a head-count) almost half an hour to make his selection of around four hundred women standing forward to be sent to their deaths.

When he'd finished he approached Irma again. 'I thought you said there were one thousand and twelve women?'

'That's correct,' she replied.

'Well, the two guards and I only counted one thousand and ten.'

Immediately Irma realised two prisoners were hiding somewhere, probably under a bed; so, without hesitation, she turned on her heals and trotted back to the vacated women's barrack with her dog. Inside she untethered Khan, who knew exactly what duty was expected of him; he sprang away excitedly from her wagging his tail inquisitively in a nose-to-ground search. It wasn't long before the dog stopped, stuck his head into the black shadows beneath a stack of three wooden bunks and began an intense nasal flurry of sniffs. Grese went to the animal, crouched down to the underside of the timber-scaffold bed and spoke into the invisible blackness. 'You'd better come out now or I'll set the dog on you,' she ordered into thin air. First the woman she'd struck with her whip at the work party crawled out, then a young girl whose face she seemed to recognise with a strange fondness, an at-odds reaction which evoked better judgement and restrained her from issuing more spiteful corporal punishment with her whip. But whatever clemency she might've felt for the girl, two women had been counted as missing so the pair must be taken back to Mengele.

Outside Mengele ordered the two women to strip naked. He told the guards to take all those women standing forward from the orderly crowd straight to the gas chambers and told the two Irma had found hiding to join them.

'You can't send these two,' Grese said, gesturing at the pair the dog had sniffed out.

The woman she'd earlier struck with the whip looked confused yet grateful; her lips rose with a simmering smile of relief. However, the poor young girl was shaking and terrified.

'Why not?' the Doctor asked curiously. 'Although the girl has blond hair, she's still a fucking Jew.'

Irma looked affectionately at the girl and felt that strange affinity warm her bosom again; but she'd never laid eyes on her before, so had to think quickly. 'I use the girl as a personal valet. She's very good at it and I could start to train her for my work-party as she'll soon be big enough to help out.'

'And the woman?' queried Mengele.

'She's already in my work-party.' Irma thought quickly for an explanation. 'She's a hard worker and qualified as a civil engineer.'

Looking at the wounds on the woman's face, the Doctor said, 'But I saw you whip her earlier on.'

'That was about something else,' explained Grese assuredly. 'It had nothing to do with her work ability.'

Mengele sighed. 'Very well, we'll compromise. The woman stays but the girl goes.'

*

Once Mengele had left the scene to pursue some other inhumane activity (he skulked like Death himself around Auschwitz), Irma Grese followed the guards who were rifle-jabbing the head-down, morose march of those condemned on their final path of life - to the gas chamber. She waited until all the condemned women were shut inside the chamber of death and the escort guards had gone before talking to the gas-chamber door-guardian (another member of the SS as the Jewish Sonderkommandos were devious and couldn't be trusted with this task). She explained to him that a mistake had been made and that her valet should not be in the gas-chamber. Although the door-guard hadn't been at the selection he knew Grese accompanied Mengele on most of them, so had no reason to doubt her. So, he dutifully unlocked the door and swung it open; Irma was inside, among the silent screams, where she quickly found the blonde-haired girl she wanted to save, because deep inside her inner-spirit sought forgiveness from the otherworld for her dubious position; mercy ought to act as compensation and an act of repentance.

"Irma Grese, this horrible creature they called the beautiful beast, she somehow — to this day, I don't know why — she saved me 16 times when Doctor (Josef) Mengele sent me to the gas chamber. She would come and take me out (of the chamber). People I spoke to who knew her said she had a sister around my age and I looked a little bit like her. The reason she saved me so many times was because I looked like her sister. That's how I survived Auschwitz." Alice Tenenbaum.

*

Time is frozen momentarily between death and resuscitation, like a dream that seems to last all night but in reality, takes just a few seconds of one's vivid imagination; or if you prefer being anaesthetized for a surgical procedure which takes hours, yet to the patient when he or she wakes, those hours seem to have disappeared into just a few seconds. Richard was still at the motorcycle crash site when the ambulance paramedics carefully removed his helmet to ensure his airway was clear; they then applied a defibrillator electric shock to his chest. Richard's heart began to beat again, but he remained cataleptic and totally unaware of pain; neither was he aware of Irma Grese, Auschwitz or anything else that'd cavorted mischievously in his sub-conscious. In fact, his mind was completely washed of any recognition to reality, both past and present. Luckily for Richard the motorist who'd found him smashed against a tree had hurried back up to the road to gain a decent reception for his mobile phone so as to make an urgent call to the emergency-services. When up there he'd spotted and flagged down an ambulance coming towards him that just happened to be returning from another crisis call-out. Those vital minutes, saved by the lucky chance of the passing paramedics, just happened to be a matter of life or death to the young curate; it also negated the need to call the police and so avoid blood-alcohol tests which they were duty-bound to undertake.

Almost a week later, Richard's bleary eyes crept open. He looked up at a bubble-like drip suspended above his hospital bed which administered a mild pain-killer, via a cannula pierced into his uninjured forearm; the other arm was encased in plaster as he'd broken both the radius and ulna bones. In addition to these injuries, he'd broken four ribs and had cracked his skull as tree-trunks have little respect for motorcycle helmets. The surgeons had also had to operate to stop a severe bleed on the temporal lobe of his brain and they were anxious to know the results of this surgery as such procedures, and possible resultant brain-damage, can cause seizures which can have epileptic and amnesia effects on an individual that can sometimes affect or alter their personality.

It was another two weeks before the surgeons were happy that his brain was healing sufficiently well for him to leave hospital with his plaster-cast arm still in a sling. After all, there'd been no seizures in his brain, and his memory (for the most-part) seemed back to normal. What the surgeons didn't know was that, as his brain healed bit by bit, his dreams when asleep were becoming more and more vivid, almost to the point of reality; they were turning to nightmares as if he was actually there at the Auschwitz death-camp (a place he knew nothing about) and they lingered and troubled his thoughts for most of the ensuing mornings. When back in the familiar comfort his bed at home, he'd been so shocked by one dream (live children been fed into flames) that he's stayed up for two nights afterwards without sleep, like the insomnia effect befalling Freddie Krueger's victims in the movie "A Nightmare on Elm Street." So, by the third evening he was completely exhausted, had drunk half a bottle of whisky and fell asleep on his sofa while watching television. Unfortunately, this close-to-coma state of fatigue provoked his inner-being to slip back in time and re-enter the psyche of Irma Grese.

As mentioned before, preincarnation pays no heed to time. Auschwitz was now churned by the buffeting, chilly winds of October 1944, the season in Poland for scurrying spiders so a resultant (and unfortunately appropriate) holocaust for flies. Irma was enjoying an evening relaxation inside the warmth of the female Aufseherin mess. Now she could be a very personable woman when she chose to be, but only towards friends and colleagues, rarely the inmates and never the Jews. On this evening she was enjoying a few glasses of schnapps with her close friend and senior ranked SS-Lagerfuhrerin (women's camp leader) Maria Mandel. Maria was thirty-two years old and, like Adolf Hitler, was Austrian by birth. She was also the highest ranked of the female guards at Auschwitz (it was her who promoted Irma to a senior guard) and was also one of the most murderous, reputedly having contributed to the deaths of over half a million women and children by the end of her brutal career.

The two were sat opposite each other at a table idly chatting when Irma brought up the subject of Sergeant Moll the Charge-Hand at the crematorium. 'I hate that man,' she said, looking Maria in the eye. 'He gives me the creeps.'

'Me too,' Mandel replied. 'Did you know it's rumoured that he once grabbed a four-year-old girl from the arms of her mother, then route-marched the little mite from the railway-carriage to the crematorium, opened the oven door and threw the child alive into the flames.'

'Oh my God!' exclaimed Irma. 'That's just terrible.' Then she smiled at Maria mockingly. 'But it's no worse than you do.'

Mandel burst a cruel chuckle. 'I hardly think so! I only authorise and sign some of the selection lists of those to be gassed.'

'But have you ever been there when the guards are pushing them inside?' asked Grese.

'Oh yes Iggy, many times. I help out and quite enjoy it actually. After all they're only Jews,' Maria replied with a sadistic sparkle alight in her eyes. 'How about you?' she asked.

'I never have,' said Irma, lying to hide the time she'd saved Alice Tenenbaum (and one or two other children she'd felt an affinity with) from death. She was sure that the inherent maternal streak of Maria's nature would understand but it was better to be safe than sorry and keep the secret to herself - just in case! 'However, from time to time I tell Josef who I think should be selected and he's always very obliging.' The pair cackled like a couple of witches at this remark, swigged back some schnapps before Irma started to appear troublesomely serious. 'Maria, I need your advice.'

Mandel smiled inquisitively. 'How can I help?'

'I've missed my period,' Irma said, matter-of-factly.

Maria raised her eyebrows. 'Do you think you're pregnant?' she asked.

'I may be,' Irma replied.

'Whose is it?'

'I can't be sure but it might be Josef's.' She looked at Maria earnestly, 'I don't want to keep it as I've got my eyes on another man now. Can you help?'

Mandel paused for thought. 'Yes, there's a Jewish woman I've seen who's a gynaecologist and who sometimes works in Josef's lab and the sanatorium. I can ask her to have a look at you.'

'Thank you,' said Grese gratefully. 'But isn't it forbidden for Jews to lay hands on Germans?'

'Officially yes, but it happens from time to time because some Jews are trained as nurses and doctors and are sometimes required to help out in the sanatorium.'

Irma still looked concerned. 'But if Baer finds out I've had an abortion done by a Jew I'd probably be whipped and lose my job.' Irma screwed her face fretfully, 'I need the money I earn here as I'm saving up for acting school for after the war.'

'Well, we'll make sure he doesn't find out,' said Maria. 'Of course, you or I won't say anything so that only leaves the gynaecologist. Just threaten to shoot her if she breathes a word to anyone. I'll do the same then she'll be doubly dead!'

Grese was amused by Mandel's last remark and her spirits lifted slightly. The pair swallowed back their glasses of schnapps, bid each other 'goodnight' then headed for their beds, Irma hoping Mengele was not in her room but instead had gone home to be with his wife.

*

Maria Mendel had arranged for Irma to have the next day (a Saturday) off work so that investigations could be made to discover if she was pregnant or not. She accompanied Grese to the sanatorium and introduced her to Gisella Perl the gynaecologist. Gisella showed Irma into a private room, white-painted with a bed in the middle and aglow by means of bright, unshaded light bulbs.

Gisella was a naturally meek and uncomplicated woman, one who was introverted and liked to keep herself to herself; she took Maria Mendel's murderous threat very seriously. She also noticed the pistol strapped around Irma's waist. She was not the type to gossip and there was no way she'd let Grese's secret slip out and she assured Irma accordingly - 'please don't worry, your secret's safe with me'.

'Would you mind sitting on the bed?' she asked Irma. The German did as requested; then Gisella looked at her nervously and began to ask questions. 'Now there are some symptoms associated with pregnancy.' She offered Irma a compassionate smile, one from Jew to German that Grese stubbornly chose not to reflect. 'Have you been having more headaches than usual recently?'

'Yes, I have,' Irma replied. 'Although I put them down to the stress of working here.'

'Have you been feeling tired and fatigued?' Gisella asked.

'Yes, that too. Sometimes I'm absolutely exhausted.'

Perl continued. 'Have you noticed any swelling of your ankles or your hands?'

Irma examined her hands, turning them over and over. 'I can't say that I have but my hands do look a bit puffier than usual.'

'And how about pain in your breasts? Are they more tender than usual?'

Grese began to massage her bosom. 'Yes, they feel more sensitive than usual.'

'Then I would say you're definitely expecting,' said Gisella. 'There's a hormone we women produce when pregnant called Human Chorionic Gonadotropin. All the symptoms you're experiencing are a result of that hormone.' She looked at Irma assuredly. 'There are a few gynaecological tests I can undertake to check, and if you are pregnant, I can perform the abortion straight away if you like?'

The tests proved that Irma Grese was pregnant and she agreed for the abortion to be undertaken immediately.

The tiny foetus was only a few weeks old, the first Aryan victim of the Auschwitz death camp.

"If a mother can kill her own child - what is left for me to kill you and you to kill me? - there is nothing between." - Mother Teresa

"It serves me right for putting all my eggs in one bastard." - Dorothy Parker

CHAPTER 4

"After thousands and thousands of dreams, we awaken. After thousands and thousands of births, we are born. This, the end, is only the beginning."- Dr Brian Weiss

Irma Grese took a few days off following the abortion as she was tender down-below and needed to rest. She told Maria that if anyone asked about her whereabouts, she was to tell them that she had flu. Mendel also agreed to feed and exercise Irma's dog. However, Doctor Mengele came to see her every evening causing her to feign the symptoms of the virus; but he did not sleep with her as he feared catching her germs; were he to be infected by her bug, the result may put in jeopardy his work in the laboratory and, more importantly, that at the gas-chamber selections; he simply couldn't put those blissfully enjoyable tasks at risk; after all, murdering Jews and Gypsies was far more fun than sex.

But Irma loved her job and was back at it after just three days of convalescence. However, she was having second thoughts about the abortion and was stewed emotionally by acid hormones resulting from the termination (a motherly instinct at odds with itself) and now resented the whole wretched process. Of course, she realised there was no going back so she was miserable and consequently in a thunderously bad mood brought about by a tinge of postnatal depression. After getting Khan from his cage, she proceeded to her charge at the Hungarian Jewesses quarters, pistol and whip strapped within her belt. It was quite a cold day but Mengele had bought her a get-well-soon present, not chocolates but a black leather trench coat which clung sensually to her curvy femininity and which somehow added a sinister aspect to her beauty; but pleasingly for Irma the chill diluted the acrid stench which had previously been agitated and intensified during the summer months by the heat of the simmering sun.

When she and the dog walked into the voluminous, stinky and nauseating gloom that festered one of the dormitory blocks, a sweat-polluted ambience that groped with echoed whispers, she noticed a scrofulous young woman squatted almost to the floor and urinating into a bucket. Grese hurried up to her, past hundreds of fretful gazes, switched her grasp on Khan's leash and withdrew her whip like a gun-fighter.

'You dirty Jewish cow!' she screamed angrily at the woman, striking her several times with her whip across her face and breasts, cruelly ignoring her victim's screams of pain.

The poor woman fell in a crumpled heap to the floor, tipping over the bucket and splashing urine over Irma's boots. 'You disgusting Jew bitch!' Grese yelled, rage peaked at the sobbing and badly bleeding curled-up woman baying like a beaten dog beneath her feet. She then lashed her target twice more, 'Why don't you use the latrines like everyone else?' she asked, shouting angrily.

The plaintive woman tried to answer between blubs which hiccupped in her throat like a nervous stutter. 'It....smells....so....bad....in....there....and....I'm....always....sick.'

Irma looked down at the woman defiantly. 'Well, you know what your next job is then.' She gave the Jew a spiteful grin. 'You've got to clean them out and it must be done today.' Grese turned to leave adding, 'I'll be back to check you've done it later on.' She then turned back and lasered a harsh stare at the woman who was trying to get to her feet. 'Understand that if they're not done the consequences for you will be very severe,' she said, wiping the woman's blood off her whip onto the clothing of another inmate.

Irma felt no guilt over what she'd just done, in fact she'd enjoyed herself and it took her mind off the abortion and those consequent foreign juices which angrily flushed her sentiments. Now she was heading for the SS laundry rooms where two young Jewish women (the Glissen sisters) worked; gullibly sensitive girls whom Irma enjoyed tormenting whenever possible, like the school bully.

On the way she crossed paths with Doctor Mengele who stopped to talk to her, cap-peak shadowing his eyes. 'My, my...I like the coat, very becoming.' He said, ogling her curves lecherously. 'I'm glad to see you're out and about and feeling better,' he continued, smiling fondly at her while inhaling a cloud of cigarette smoke that swirled in his mouth like a whirlwind. 'Will you be attending the selection this evening?'

'I don't think so Josef, I'm not really feeling up to it yet.'

'That's a shame,' replied the doctor looking disappointed, his words spewing out in misty bubbles of smoke. 'If there's anyone in particular you'd like me to pick out just let me know.' He paused briefly for thought. 'How about some children?'

Irma looked at him thoughtfully; the murdering of children was something she found distasteful and simply couldn't reason with, that feminine conscience provoked at the thought of cutting short a budding life. 'Although there are hundreds of new prisoners in the blocks I supervise, there are no children as the guards now seem to take them straight from the train to the gas chambers.' She sighed plaintively, thinking to herself that she could've been a mother in a few months' time; a woman's exclusive right denied her by Nazism. 'It seems to me there's something particularly wicked about taking young lives, so select as many old women as you can as they've lived a long life and are quite useless at work.'

'I've seen plenty of children around Don't you remember the one you found hiding in the block a couple of months back?'

Irma pictured young Alice Tenenbaum in her mind's eye. She'd moved the girl to a different woman's barrack, a place where she wouldn't be so easily noticed and where selections were less frequent because all those housed within its muttering walls worked at the camp. 'Yes, I do,' she answered. 'But she was the only one I've seen and she's dead now.'

'Well, have you any other ideas?' asked Mengele.

'I would choose the pretty ones if I were you.'

'Why?' queried Mengele. 'Looking as good as you do, surely you can't be envious?'

'No, I'm not,' she answered, matter-of-factly. 'It's just that I've noticed some of our guards fraternising and flirting with them and we can't be expected to encourage such behaviour.'

'Yes, I take your point,' the doctor said gravely. 'The pretty ones and the old women are on the menu for this evening then.' He smiled again, 'Anyway Iggy, I'm in a bit of a hurry: got to see Baer but I might pop over to yours later.'

*

It had started to spit with rain as Irma and Khan approached the laundry. She looked up at the heavy, blackening sky falling down like a roller blind, dropped the dog's lead, turned up the collar of her coat, ducked her head inside it and wrapped the lapels up to her eyes.

She then began to run towards the entrance and Khan trotted along obediently in her wake. Suddenly the rainfall intensified to torrents, splashing dust to mud like seething lava pools while great plumes of black smoke spewed out from the five crematoria brick funnels, the rain spiralling flakes of bone-meal onto the many roofs of Auschwitz like a snow blizzard. Despite the conditions, elsewhere in the camp all the inmate work-parties kept labouring at their chores, toiling hard while their guards and their dogs took shelter.

Irma hurried into the laundry (the dog followed), unbuttoned her coat and shook off the raindrops. She looked for the Glissen girls around this large room with several people working industrially, ironing SS uniforms and shirts, throwing sheets and pillow-cases into and atop the yawning mouths of many whirling washing machines; it was a coloured carnival of labour. The sisters usually worked together and she spotted one of them spinning the handle of a wooden-roller clothes wrangler. The girl saw Irma approach, stood respectfully to attention and tried to look pleased and welcoming and immune to the nerves that churned in her gut; she was terrified of the German as she'd once witnessed her beating a workmate with her whip.

When Grese reached the young Jewess, she took the riding-crop from her belt and slapped it threateningly against her boot. She then gave the girl a dismissive glance and said, 'Do you know what will happen to you when the war is over and Germany rules this world?'

The girl shook her dispirited visage negatively.

Grese began to tease her, prodding Glissen's left breast with the whip. There was malicious pleasure alight in Irma's eyes like a snake before the strike. 'Let me tell you then,' she said, grinning spitefully. 'All Jews, that includes all the men, women and children that are left alive, are going to be sterilised to put an end to your treacherous race of people.' She began to stroke the tip of her whip across the girl's face. 'And you'll all be deported to East Africa to work in German factories which we will build there; and during your free time you'll be slaves in German households.' Irma eyed the girl conspiringly. 'I might go there myself when the war's over and take you and your fucking sister as my slaves.' Noticing the Jew had turned as white as a sheet, was wide-eyed and trembling like a leaf, Irma felt a pang of guilt over her taunting so decided to cease as she knew the young woman (who happened to be just a few months older than herself) had tried to commit suicide a couple of times beforehand. Besides it didn't seem fair to take her postnatal misery out on another woman when a man (Doctor Mengele) should take the brunt of the blame.

*

That evening Irma was sat in the female mess drinking schnapps with and talking to the garrulous Maria Mandel who suddenly raised the subject of the allied forces invasion progress. 'Did you know that the Russian army is closing in on us?' she asked Irma.

'I'd heard rumours,' Grese replied, emitting a dejected sigh. 'Josef is very worried about it but I can't imagine that Adolf Hitler will allow the situation to escalate.'

Maria replied. 'The trouble is that, now the Americans and Russians have joined the allies, we're out-numbered and having to fight on both the east and west fronts.' She gave Irma a watery-eyed worried look. 'I'm just not sure how long we can hold out.'

Irma was good at being supportive when needed. She reached across the table, placed her hand on Maria's and gave a reassuring smile. 'I'm quite sure we'll be safe and you shouldn't worry so much.'

'Let's hope you're right Iggy, because there is talk of abandoning this camp and sending us to other ones in Germany where it'll be safer.'

Irma now had a comical twinkle in her eyes to lift the sullen moment. 'They should let us girls do the fighting; we'd soon win the war.' She then changed subject as it was disturbing to dwell upon the probability of Germany's gloomy destiny. 'Anyway, how was your day? How many did you manage to send to the gas chambers?'

'Well over four thousand today. Baer wants the whole process speeded up just in case the Red Army gets here. If that turns out to be the case, those prisoners that are left here will be marched to camps in Germany.' Maria sighed deeply, shaking her head despondently, 'Baer has already started to destroy paperwork and other records so obviously he's taking the threat very seriously.'

*

Richard Pope bolted awake from this nightmare. Who on Earth was that military woman he'd been speaking to in German he'd somehow translated in the reverie but now didn't understand? Why was his memory of the dream only visual and his thoughts befuddled by German gobbledegook he didn't comprehend? And why did every horrid dream seem so real? Oh, dear God what was happening to him?

That vibrant light of springtime bounced into the room from a split between the drawn curtains, so he glanced across at an alarm clock. Half past nine! Curses it was Sunday morning and he only had an hour to get ready and arrive at the church as stand-in for the Reverend Clotworthy. Richard slowly slung himself out of bed, his head still throbbing from the copious amount of whisky he'd drank the previous evening. It was not the recollection of an abusive childhood that now made him drink himself to sleep; it was currently the horrors he witnessed in his dreams.

Richard still hadn't replaced his motorcycle so, after a brief shower and then getting dressed, he ordered a taxi which got him to the church for ten fifteen. This was late for him and most of the congregation was already queued on the gravel approach waiting for him to unlock the entrance. The deacon panted a few hurried apologies along the queue as he hurried to the door and opened it. He then went straight to the vestry, donned his cassock and surplice, swung a stole around his neck while his entire congregation filtered slowly into the pews, most tethered by the creaky old bones of advanced age.

Deacon Richard Pope then left the vestry to address his audience. Standing in the chancel just a few feet ahead of the altar, he smiled welcomingly and begun his address. 'A very good morning to you all and, may I say, how pleasing it is to see so many of you here.' He looked around the entire nave full of people, other than those hidden in shadows behind stone pillars. 'As I'm sure most of you are aware next Friday is Good Friday so let us pray.' Richard clutched his hands (forearm still in plaster) and closed his eyes, 'Almighty and everlasting God, who stooped to raise fallen humanity through the child-bearing of blessed Mary: grant that we, who have seen your glory revealed in our human nature and your love made perfect in our weakness, may daily be renewed in your image and conformed to the pattern of your Son Jesus Christ our Lord, who is alive and reigns with you, in the unity of the Holy Spirit, one God, now and forever.' He opened his eyes again. 'We'll begin today's service with Hymn number three five one.'

The deacon sang cheerily along with the congregation. When it was over, and after traditional prayers and lamented-psalms, a middle-aged woman wearing an absurd frilly hat read the first lesson from the Bible. Then another hymn, some more tedious prayers and Richard read the second lesson.

It was almost forty minutes before he could deliver his sermon stood aloft in the ornately carved wooden pulpit. Once up there he pulled out four sheets of paper from his cassock pocket, spread them over a paper-stand lectern and begun, speaking clearly and confidentially. 'Now, as it's so close to Easter I'd like to speak to you about the miracle of Jesus' rising up from the dead and his ascension into Heaven.'

Unexpectedly he froze, the colour drained from his face and he stopped delivering the sermon, his eyes suddenly wide like saucers. He was experiencing a brain spasm trance resulting from the head injury and was stood stagnant like a marble bust as the colour drained from his face. He was suffering an out-of-body experience as the congregation looked at him anxiously wondering what was wrong.

Thirty seconds…One minute…Two - then suddenly an animated explosion of activity from the deacon. Although unconscious and dazed, Richard began to preach another sermon, not the one he'd prepared. And he began bullishly, delivering it with uncharacteristic gusto; an oration to his horror-struck onlookers of something he somehow subconsciously translated to English from Irma's memory of an Adolf Hitler speech.

'My feelings as a Christian point me to my Lord and Saviour as a fighter. It points me to the man who once in loneliness, surrounded only by a few followers, recognized these Jews for what they were and summoned men to fight against them and who, God's truth, was greatest not as a sufferer but as a fighter.'

Richard looked wildly up at the rafters and his rant intensified. It didn't even sound like him, was as if he'd been possessed by some gravel-voiced demon. And the mien among those gathered before him was one of agape and troubled astonishment.

'In boundless love as a Christian and as a man I read through the passage which tells us how the Lord at last rose in His might and seized the scourge to drive out of the Temple the brood of vipers and adders. How terrific was His fight for the world against the Jewish poison? To-day, after two thousand years, with deepest emotion I recognize more profoundly than ever before in the fact that it was for this that He had to shed His blood upon the Cross.'

His rant now escalated to a rallying call and many in his audience recognised this Nazi subject and Richard's Fuhrer-like mannerism.

'As a Christian I have no duty to allow myself to be cheated, but I have the acting rightly it is the distress that daily grows. For as a Christian I have also a duty to my own people. I believe that I am acting in accordance with the will of the Almighty Creator: by defending myself against the Jew, I am fighting for the work of the Lord. Amen.'

Then Richard collapsed in a heap inside the pulpit and two women from the congregation rushed up to help him.

*

It was now November 1944 back at Auschwitz and bone-meal sullied snow, patterned by millions of footprints, carpeted the ground in the complex. Irma, wearing her black leather trench-coat, was excitedly on her way to Doctor Mengele's lab, because the woman she'd caught peeing into a bucket was having her breasts removed as the whip wounds Irma had inflicted had become horribly infected due to the punishment of having to clean-out the filthy toilet block.

Before joining the SS, Irma had trained to become a nurse and was fascinated by all medical matters and procedures; so, this was an operation she simply couldn't miss as Mengele was attempting to graft the amputation wounds with the skin from a recently deceased corpse, an experiment which would save his patient (or should that be victim) from the gas chambers. However, septicaemia had already set in and she would die a few days later.

Inside Mengele's lab were the doctor himself and two SS men guarding his pitiable patient. When Irma entered the premises, the Jewess was already stripped naked and securely strapped down on a cold, stainless-steel operating table, her lacerated breasts inflamed, red and oozing with pus, her eyes almost popping out by the anticipated terror of what was to come. Although weakened by a tide of sepsis swilling throughout her body, the woman was frantically wriggling for freedom and Irma felt a pang of guilt and slightly squeamish over the awful infected state of the wounds she'd inflicted.

After the doctor had stubbed out a cigarette, he noticed that Grese had arrived on the scene; so, he flashed her a welcoming smile. He was ready for surgery and wearing a white laboratory coat, plastic apron and rubber gloves.

He spoke to Irma from across the room. 'You're just in time Iggy, I was about to start without you.' He then raised a surgical mask from beneath his chin to cover his mouth and nose and then picked up a scalpel from a sterilisation kidney dish.

Irma moved over to the operating table opposite Mengele who was concentrating on the patient's left breast. He touched and flicked the nipple causing the Jewess to wince with pain as she tightened her grip on the table-edge, tense knuckles bleached of blood. This amused Mengele as he approached the base of the patient's left breast with his scalpel, his target's face screwed with the anticipated dread of one facing the torturer.

Noticing the terror on the Jew's face, Irma looked at the doctor with open-mouthed disbelief. 'Surely, you're not going to operate without putting her to sleep?' she asked, slightly concerned for the woman's welfare despite the fact she, Irma Grese, was the cause of the surgery.

Mengele looked up from his focus. 'I'm not going to anesthetise her,' he said, his words muffled by his mask. 'She's a Jew and I can't spare the ether.'

He then made the first bloody incision which Irma found strangely thrilling. This barbaric butchering was horrendously wicked, the victim whimpering in agony as threads of blood poured from the doctor's slicing scalpel, cutting around the base of the breast, cutting inwards and severing it deliberately slowly to torment the woman who eventually passed out from the pain. Blood poured in rivulets onto the operating table then spilt onto the floor forming a viscous slick of crimson globules. Once the breast was removed, he cut off the other one, replicating the torturous leisureliness of the first amputation, an evil grimace twisting his face like that mirrored on the fascinated visage of Irma Grese. Then he took the skin he'd earlier removed from a cyanide-gas polluted corpse, roughly cut it to size then grafted it over the open wounds using stitches which he purposely sunk slowly and deliberately deep.

"And she felt the beauty in the music now, drank it in with tears streaming down her face. Never had she been so naked in worship before her Creator, allowing the adoration to bleed out her very fingertips onto the strings, playing her heart's cry for every single lost soul, for the loss of innocence every generation to come would possess as a result of what happened at the killing fields of Auschwitz." - Kristy Cambron

CHAPTER 5

Richard had ended up in hospital again after the outrage in the church. Despite a bucket of water and gentle slaps to his face, no one had been able to wake him from unconsciousness. Two of the male members of the congregation managed to feet-and-hands stretcher him out of the building to a car and then drove him to Accident and Emergency. It was while sat in the waiting room that Richard finally woke up, his memory completely oblivious to the ranting Nazi-like sermon he'd given a couple of hours earlier. One of the two men who accompanied him to the hospital sympathetically explained why he was there (to Richard's confused amnesia) and advised that while here he ought to see a specialist. The anxious deacon readily agreed and was eventually escorted by a male nurse to the neurology department and thoroughly examined by a neurologist (brain-expert doctor.) As a result of Richard's medical history and brain-damage from the motorcycle accident, the medic explained that he'd most likely suffered an epileptic brain-seizure and prescribed a course of drugs (carbamazepine) to combat the effects of the condition. He also told him that it was a legal obligation to inform the vehicle and driving authority about his diagnosis and that he must also take a few days off work to rest.

Richard spent a few relatively untroubled days convalescing at home and had no nightmares about Auschwitz to agitate his sleep. However, once word of his shameful sermon reached the ears of other clerics within the diocese, the bishop became extremely concerned about the young deacon's welfare. So, Richard was summoned to a meeting with the bishop where he apologised profusely for his uncharacteristic behaviour and explained (to his divine superior) about the lack of sleep due to awful nightmares he'd suffered since the motorcycle accident. It was a difficult situation for the bishop to deal with simply because Richard was ill and the Church couldn't ask him to leave his position because of his deviant behaviour, something which the poorly young man clearly had no control over. On the other hand, the prelate daren't risk the likelihood of another Nazi-like outburst from the pulpit so Richard would be suspended from duties for the time being; however, he could keep his job on full salary providing he agreed to attend a psychiatrist for analysis and additional treatment, a course of therapy which the Church would fund.

*

The doctor of psychiatry appointed by the Church had learned everything (chapter and verse) from the Bishop of what had happened to Richard and about the brain injury he'd recently sustained. He was a gentleman called Tony Ludlow, a portly man in his late fifties who always wore smart suits or tweed jackets to work. He was also a soft-spoken and extremely courteous man with a horseshoe of tufty, silver-hair encircling his naked scalp and a sharp beak-like nose propped onto which were half-moon spectacles. Inside Ludlow's therapy room, an ambience which bounced with affluent splendour, Richard was sunk in the lavish comfort of a leather armchair and the doctor eyed him studiously from over the tortoise-shell rim of his glasses.

'Welcome young man,' said the psychiatrist, smiling warmly. 'Before we start, I wish to assure you that anything you tell me remains within these walls. Now, I'm going to be giving you a few sessions of what we call cognitive behavioural therapy because I've been informed that you've been suffering from a great deal of anxiety since that unfortunate motorcycle accident.' Ludlow offered an assuring smile, 'Now the bishop has told me what happened at the church. Can you elaborate and tell me anymore about this incident?'

'I've been told something of what happened,' Richard replied, a worried look on his face. 'One woman from the congregation even filmed me in action on her phone.' Sadness moistened his troubled eyes. 'That's not me on the film; I would never say things like that.'

'But can you remember anymore? like what brought it on?'

'No, I afraid I can't remember anything about it, only the brief clip that I've seen on that lady's phone.'

'I see,' said Ludlow looking puzzled. 'I asked the Bishop to make sure you brought your patient notes from the hospital. Did you remember them?'

Richard reached inside the tartan lining of his Barbour jacket and withdrew a brown envelope which he handed across to the doctor.

Ludlow then unfolded the notes, spread them over his knee and peered down at them through his glasses. 'It says here that you probably suffered an epileptic brain-seizure.' He paused and scratched his forehead. 'Extraordinary! I'm not an expert on the subject but I thought people who suffered from epilepsy always collapsed while having a tonic clonic fit.' He looked up at Richard, 'Do you mind if I have a word with the neurologist who treated you at hospital? His name and the neurology section's telephone number are on these notes and he may be able to give me some clues as to which kind of cognitive therapy would be most beneficial and effective for you.'

'Not at all,' Richard willingly agreed.

'I'll do that now,' said Tony Ludlow as he rose from his chair. He then left the room closing the door behind him.

The doctor returned about five minutes later and once again sat opposite Richard. 'I managed to get hold of the neurologist,' he confirmed, nodding his head. He then hesitated for thought. 'He said that it was extremely rare, but not unheard of, to have the kind of seizure you experienced. He was extremely helpful and has given me good advice on how to conduct your therapy.' He looked at the deacon compassionately, 'Since you can't remember what happened in the church, it sounds to me as if you're suffering with what's known as dissociative identity disorder which usually stems back to experiences or trauma during childhood, so I'd like to begin with that....'

The psychiatrist had already gained the trust of Richard Pope simply because of client confidentiality and the fact he was desperate to get better and return to work; if that involved getting things off his chest, then so be it! So, he began to tell the story of his dreadful upbringing, beginning with how his father lured him to bed every morning when his mother was downstairs making breakfast. The abuse probably began when the boy was around four years old, too long ago for Richard to fully remember every detail; but he recalled climbing up into bed alongside his father, enticed by interesting stories that flowed from his father's ingratiating lips or sometimes interesting science and geology sets to study; but moreover, the boy was summoned by the fear of angry repercussions were he not to keep up with the routine. It was while his father was reading to him that large, rough hands invaded into Richard's privacy, unbuttoning his pyjama bottoms and playing with his cuckoo (as his father referred to the genital area.) And sometimes the scary man would show Richard his cuckoo which was large and stiff and which made the poor lad feel extremely uncomfortable and want to run away into the sanctuary of his mother's arms.

One morning the young Richard was struck by an epiphany and suddenly realised that this was not the conduct of a loving parent; his father's behaviour was disgusting and it was wrong and one day, when he was older, he would tell Mummy exactly what had been going on. Would she believe him? Did she have suspicions? Richard doubted it because for her it was like walking on glass with her husband's unpredictable moods when trouble was lurking in the house; he could flick from oily charm to outrageous anger like a switch, and telling her would likely cause more turmoil, a storm of motherly protection to educe his rage. If she ever dared to protest over anything, his belligerent and patronising manner towards the poor woman always evoked her tear-jerked and immediate surrender. But in the end, there was no need to tell Mummy as boarding school came to his rescue.

And then there were those awful educational years. If anyone thought bullying was a thing of the past, they'd be mistaken. Bullies can still push their victims into dark cupboards, away from authoritative eyes to slap and punch them; upturn their beds when they're asleep; purposely foul them on the football pitch or whack them with a cricket bat. The young Richard had suffered every indignity when he'd first attended school. Of course, as he grew bigger and stronger the bullies began to leave him alone; such is the characteristic creed of the coward. But something he didn't tell the psychiatrist was that, over and above all this, he harboured a guilty conscience about the copious amounts of alcohol he used to medicate these nightmares of his dreadful childhood and more recently the awful dreams about cruel Germans which pommelled inside his reasoning like a violent banshee.

*

After the session with Doctor Ludlow, Richard returned to his little apartment, his mind agitated by what he'd told the psychiatrist. It was not the trouble-shared-trouble-halved result he'd hoped for, it was a festering trauma of reliving his childhood and reigniting those vivid memories; so, he drank the afternoon away, eventually going to bed in a drunken stupor around eight o'clock. He fell straight asleep and was back as Irma Grese who'd finished dressing into her uniform and was looking at Josef Mengele who was sat up and bare-chested in her bed. In private Irma wanted to end this relationship because she'd fallen for another man, an SS Oberscharfuhrer (squad leader) by the name Franz Hatzinger (a married man fourteen years her senior) who was also stationed at Auschwitz. Franz was caring and compassionate towards her and had none of the brash indifference Mengele so often demonstrated. The trouble was that she couldn't really ditch Mengele in favour of her new beau, because the doctor outranked him and such treachery might lead to woeful, Mengele-revenge consequences for both her and Franz. So, their sexual relationship was not the most romantic imaginable and had to be conducted in secret, usually in his quarters if no one was around; and intercourse had to be quick for fear of getting caught and usually carried out fully clothed and up against an uncomfortable wall.

Mengele drew her attention by clearing his throat ready to speak. 'I'm going to the camp's railway station at nine this morning to help the guards and officers make a selection from there. Would you care to join me?'

'No thank you Josef,' she quickly replied. 'I hate it there; to watch guards shoot children in the head at point-blank range. I don't have the stomach for that.'

'Really?' questioned the doctor. 'It doesn't bother me in the least.' He hesitated for thought. 'Well, I'll be in my lab around noon if you'd care to come along.'

'Alright Josef, I'll see you there,' she awkwardly confirmed, guilty of her secret shared only with Franz.

It was now early January at the death camp and bitterly cold, wintry-sharp with glistening icicles hanging from gutters and window-sills. Every puddle was glazed with ice and the frosted mud underfoot was as hard as rock; the chill, prickly and frozen by a bleak and tearing bitterness. But Auschwitz writhed with busy, trying-to-keep-warm, work-party activity; all shivering under an insipid, cloudless sky which was blotched only by the black bone-meal smoke that billowed out of the crematoria chimneys. Even the guards, squeezed hands-in-pockets into warm coats (a luxury denied the prisoners), were more animated than usual and trying to keep warm, flurried trots on the spot while their breaths whited like recumbent ghosts. After slipping into her leather trench-coat, Irma got her dog and then began her daily routine, flushing thousands of Hungarian Jewesses out from the stewed, body-warm ambience of their quarters, outside into the Arctic-like conditions. Once assembled, she and other rifle-wielding guards made them parade naked and shivering like agitated jellies while she took a roll-call. Grese was purposely sluggish with this task taking almost an hour to count each individual block she had charge over.

By the time she'd finished it was past noon so she headed for Mengele's lab. She tethered the frost-panting dog to a post outside the laboratory where three skeletally thin, rope-bound naked men lay on the ice-hard ground, shivering their skin-wrapped bones like cold fish wriggling away life on the river-bank. This was something she'd seen many times before, derived from an experiment to measure the lowest temperatures the human body could withstand. Mengele and Heinrich Himmler had masterminded the technique a couple of years beforehand to help save the lives of German troops fighting the Russians on the freezing eastern front. Of course, Jews were the guinea pigs, usually in larger groups than just three, and when only one remained alive he or she would be carried inside to experiment upon the best method to warm them up until fully revived. If the victim survived this process, he or she was shot so they couldn't blabber-mouth to others. They'd found that warming someone's body in a hot bath had the best results but, because the ice-men Russians and Siberian temperatures had defeated the ill-equipped German armies, the need for experimenting was now unnecessary; so, this wicked procedure had just become a winter game to amuse the doctor's deviant sense of humour.

Irma went inside the lab and found Mengele, attired in his white laboratory coat, behind some medical cabinets. He was holding a syringe of dark liquid in his rubber-gloved hand and was crouched-down facing a small, tubby boy who was brutally restrained from wriggling by a guard standing behind him. The youngster stood just a head higher than the guard's belt, so would have been around ten-years-old; his mouth agape and gagged by a screwed-up cloth; his left eye forced wide open by a wire clamp, so much so that it protruded grotesquely and looked ready to pop out. Because he was bursting with flesh Irma took an instant dislike to him. *It seemed unfair to her that he was plump and well-nourished while most of the other children in the camp were just starved bags of skin and bones who had to ferret around for filthy scraps to eat. *(in this case the podgy boy and his parents had been found by Belgium SS troops, caught taking refuge in the back of a shoemaker's shop in Antwerp. The Jewish family - the parents, the fat boy and his two elder sisters - were herded onto the transport system which eventually arrived at Auschwitz; the protesting shoemaker and his apple-pie wife were shot and left in the street).

Irma gave the doctor a gentle kiss on his cheek then savagely slapped the boy across his chubby face, reddening it like a tomato. With her attention back on Mengele, she asked, 'What are you going to do to this fat Jewish brat?'

There was a cruel sneer twisting the doctor's mouth as he answered. 'I've had many fairly successful attempts to try and change the colour of the eye's iris but only on those I've plucked out of dead bodies. However, the results have been blotchy which I think's due to the optic-nerve being severed from the brain. I've tried to have a go on the living but they all struggled awkwardly and preferred to be shot...stupid Jews.' There was a menacing pleasure now alight in his eyes.' I found this fat, weak boy on the transport this morning. As he has green snake-eyes and I'm going to attempt to change their colour to Jewish black using squid-ink.' He looked down at the boy again. 'Head up please,' he said, giving the child an unctuous grimace. The guard holding the lad grabbed the youngster's scalp and viciously yanked back his head, holding it as still as stone. The boy winced from the pain and was sweating with dread as Mengele crouched over him and approached his eyeball with the syringe. The doctor focused-in on his target and tears of anguish from the unclamped eye streamed down the boy's chubby cheeks as the needle got closer and closer to its' target. When the syringe touched the eye, Mengele teased the boy by prodding his cornea with the tip of the needle then, with one swift stab he pierced the iris and the gag shot out of the child's shrieking mouth like a bullet.

*

Richard bolted awake, wide-eyed and terrified. There was half-a-glass of unfinished whisky on his bed-side cabinet which he grabbed and swigged back like a parched man from the desert sun. That had been the worst nightmare he'd yet experienced and as vivid as watching some dreadful horror movie. So, he got out of bed, drew back the curtains and sunshine burst into the room, slapping his hangover headache like a bully. He then put on a dressing gown and some slippers and headed for a whisky bottle floundering on the floor by the sofa in the lounge; he poured himself a large drink then sat, picked up his mobile phone and finger pointed the contact window on the screen.

Although it was still quite early in the morning, Tony Ludlow answered almost immediately and then Richard spoke sounding fretful and extremely anxious. 'Hello Mr Ludlow, its Richard Pope here.'

'Hello Richard, how can I help?'

'I've just had the most terrible nightmare. Please Mr Ludlow,' he implored, 'I need your help.'

After a pitiful yelp, Tony replied. 'Of course, Mr Pope, that's my job. Why don't you come to see me at eleven this morning and I'll ask a colleague of mine if he'll also attend?'

'Thank you, I'll be there.' Richard hung-up and gulped down his glass of whisky.

*

Having taken a taxi into town, Richard arrived at the psychiatry surgery a couple of minutes after eleven, sucking a strong mint to disguise the pungent smell of alcohol on his breath. He spoke to the receptionist who buzzed through to Ludlow's consulting room. Moments later the doctor's office door swung open and the psychiatrist gestured for Richard to enter with a welcoming smile ingratiating his face. As he passed into the room Ludlow greeted him warmly and Richard sat where he had on the previous occasion; but this time opposite another middle-aged man who the doctor explained practised hypnotherapy and who was there to help by attempting to explore the deep caverns in Richard's troubled mind. The three of them chatted for a while and the hypnotist, a bearded man who wore jeans and a T-shirt, happily introduced himself as Martin. Richard then explained in great detail about his dream which both men found sympathetically shocking.

'Have you had many of these horrid dreams?' asked the psychiatrist.

'They're becoming more frequent,' the deacon confirmed.

'I think the only way we can stop these nightmares is with hypnotherapy,' said Ludlow. 'So, it's extremely fortuitous that Martin agreed to come along today.' (Knowing what happened to Richard in the church, it was probably not Ludlow's brightest idea to attempt to induce a trance.)

'Thank you,' replied Richard. 'I'm willing to try whatever it takes.'

'But it may not be what I'd previously diagnosed because dissociative identity disorder usually comes with amnesia blackouts; you seem to remember these dreams.' He paused for thought, 'Let's see what we can discover with hypnotherapy.' The doctor switched his attention to the hypnotist. 'Over to you then Martin,'

The man in jeans and T-shirt offered Richard a warm, assuring smile. 'Let's begin then,' he said, focusing intently on the young deacon. 'I want you to sit completely upright.' Richard stretched his torso erect; 'Now put your arms on your lap and close your eyes.' Richard did as asked; 'Very good. Now relax your muscles and breathe deeply, in through your nose and out through your mouth.' Martin paused to monitor the young man's breathing. 'Excellent. Now, using slow controlled breaths, I want you to inwardly countdown from one hundred.'

Richard, breathing deeply and slowly, began to countdown in his head; one hundred, ninety-nine, ninety-eight......You could hear a pin drop as the other two men watched him with fixed fascination. At the count of twenty-two his head flopped down.

'He's under,' the hypnotist said to Tony Ludlow. Martin then switched his attention back to the stupefied deacon. 'Richard, I want you to open your eyes.'

The young deacon's eyes snapped open; he then flicked up his head wildly like a cobra ready to strike and, without knowing it, sprang to his feet and thrust out a Nazi salute. The stunned hypnotist, mouth agape with alarmed disbelief, slapped his hands in the air frantically attempting to awaken Richard from the trance.

But the deacon was in another place and time and began another wide-eyed, ranting outburst, translated from the memory cells of Irma Grese. *'Germany should feel no guilt over the Jewish problem, without them we can build an empire greater than the British. It took England three hundred years to gradually build her Empire, and for three hundred years this World Empire was welded together solely by force.'* He flung his arms out like a mad tyrant and every attempt to restrain him failed because of the violence in his gesticulations. He then began to shout, adding a wild-eyed rage to his tirade. *'War followed war. One nation after another was robbed of its freedom. One state after another was shattered so that the structure which calls itself the British Empire might arise. British democracy is nothing but a mask covering the suppression and the oppression of nations and individuals. Concentration camps were not invented in Germany; it is the murderous English who were the ingenious inventors of this idea. By these means they contrived to break the backbone of other nations, to remove their resistance, to wear them down, and make them prepared at last to submit to this British yoke of democracy.'* Once again Richard Pope collapsed, falling back in a heap on the sofa.

Tony Ludlow looked at the hypnotist with a wide-eyed, worried and confused expression on his face. 'My God!' he exclaimed breathlessly. 'It's as if he's possessed. We better get him to hospital.'

"It is more difficult to undermine faith than knowledge, love succumbs to change less than to respect, hatred is more durable than aversion, and at all times the driving force of the most important changes in this world has been found less in a scientific knowledge animating the masses, but rather in a fanaticism dominating them and in a hysteria which drove them forward." - Adolf Hitler,

Irma's lips played tenderly with those belonging to her lover, Franz Hatzinger. They were alone together in the male guard's quarters and she was up against the wall, skirt up with her stocking shrouded legs curled around his groin, her private femininity naked beyond the elastic garter, her crotch throbbing wantonly against his open-belt nudity. Franz's strong arms held Irma up by her bottom from inside her skirt and he was pumping his manhood into her like a wild animal when Mengele walked into the room. Irma squealed with orgasmic delight as she climaxed; they were both too lustfully involved with each other (numbed by sexual senses) to notice the doctor who took a moment or two to recognise the identity of these two romping lovers.

'YOU FILTHY, TWO-TIMING FUCKING SLUT!!' he shouted angrily, face reddening as he did so. Terrified and surprised, Franz immediately released his hold on Irma and awkwardly turned away to buttoned-up his trousers.

Irma blushed shamefully as she looked at Mengele, 'It's not what looked like, Josef,' she said timidly.

'You stupid bitch,' retorted the doctor, slightly less harshly. 'Do you think I was born yesterday?' Mengele was furious inside, angered by her Perfidia treachery. He breathed deeply to calm himself (best he could) and lit a cigarette. Feeling slightly less agitated (calmed by nicotine) he said, 'The reason I've been looking for you is that Baer has received orders from Himmler to evacuate Auschwitz because the Red Army is now too close. We are taking the Jews and other prisoners to camps in Germany.' He pointed at Grese, 'You are going back to Ravensbruck.' Then he swung his finger angrily to Franz, 'And you!... you back-stabbing bastard...you are being sent to Bergen-Belsen.' He focused again on Irma, 'You're leaving today by train with all the other SS women so I'd go and get packed if I were you. It leaves from here at fourteen hundred hours and is heading towards Berlin.' He switched his attention back to Franz, 'You are to remain here as all the male guards will be transporting prisoners' on-foot to their alternative camp.' Mengele sniggered menacingly into his gloved hand, 'You've got a bloody long walk ahead of you.'

*

By now Irma had lost that coveted friendship of Maria Mandel as the woman had been posted to the Dachau concentration camp in Germany. However, Maria had introduced Grese to her replacement (a woman called Elisabeth Volkenrath) and had endorsed Irma's merits as a loyal and conscientious senior member of the women's SS. It was left to Grese to show Volkenrath around the death camp and introduce her to work colleagues including Commandant Baer. As a consequence of this, Irma found a new friendship with Elisabeth, something they enjoyed celebrating most evenings with schnapps in the female mess.

Back in her quarters Irma began to carefully place (neatly-folded-military-method) items of clothing and keep-sake mementos into two brown-leathers suitcases open on her bed. Once she'd finished, she looked fondly around the room, absorbing into her mind the many happy memories the ambience invoked. She was sorry to be leaving Auschwitz which had been her home for over twenty months and somewhere where she'd forged many friendships; however, all good things must come to an end. But Ravensbruck wasn't such a bad posting; at least it was warmer in north Germany and she'd also enjoyed her previous job working there as the treatment of prisoners wasn't quite so inhuman and the conditions were vastly more hygienic. With these thoughts in her head, she clipped closed the suitcases, pulled them off the bed (one in each hand) and then left the room. Downstairs she collected Khan from his cage, looped a leash around the handle of a suitcase then attached it to the animal's collar. Then, wrapped up warmly in her leather trench coat, she and the dog headed for the train deportation platform. Two guards saw her struggling with heavy suitcases and a dog so, lured by the seductive sway of her pear-shaped curves, they offered to help, an invitation which Irma gladly accepted.

The deportation platform was chaotic, a swarming bedlam of hundreds of prisoners emptying from the train and being barrel-jabbed into groups by machine-gun-guards and angry, snarling dogs. Bone-meal smoke wafted above and around them in pungent clouds; guards and SS officers alike shouting angry instructions this way and that; pistol shots snapped into the air one after the other, as many in the crowds slumped in lifeless mounds to the ground. It was almost two o'clock and the locomotive and cattle carriages (swapping roles – Jews out, Germans in), due to take the Aufseherin away from Auschwitz, floundered heavily by the platform seething with steam like a gasping dragon. When they reached it Irma's escort guards carefully pushed her suitcases up inside the cattle carriage, as Irma and her dog cautiously navigated a narrow and rickety ramp up inside. It was by lucky chance that Elisabeth Volkenrath was in the same carriage (along with ten other SS women) sat on her suitcase huddled-up in the corner reading a book.

Elisabeth looked up from her read. 'Hello Iggy,' she said with a pleased-to-see-you smile. 'What a coincidence for us to share the same carriage. Come and sit beside me and we can keep each other warm.'

So, using her foot, Irma slid one of the suitcases across the carriage floor and placed it alongside Elisabeth. She then sat on it and the two women nuzzled together for shared body-heat. Then the door was slid across from outside, slowly drawing in the darkness like a solar eclipse.

When it closed, timid light trickled in from a procession of slatted air-gaps along the carriage's wooden flank walls, but it was insufficient for Volkenrath to read so she put down her book and said to Irma, 'I've never asked before but I'm curious; what made you join the Schutzstaffel?'

With a seething of steam which swished into the carriage causing some of the other women to splutter and cough, the train slowly lunged forward, creaking and clanking strenuously. It was noisy but Elisabeth could hear Irma speak above the clamour. 'Well, that's a long story,' she paused for thought. 'I suppose, if I'm perfectly honest, it was probably my father who prompted my decision to enlist.'

'Why was that?' questioned Volkenrath. 'Is your father a supporter of the Nazi party?'

'Yes he is, but I joined to spite him as he's a chauvinistic pig who thinks all women should be chained to the kitchen sink and shouldn't be allowed in the army.'

Clickety clack......Clickety clack.....Clickety clack....The train was slowly gaining speed.

'He sounds like an awful man,' said Elisabeth. 'Did be bully you when you were a child?'

'Not only me,' sighed Irma. 'He bullied my mother and my sister and brothers.' Despite the gloom, Volkenrath could just about perceive shadows on Irma's face curling down ruefully from the memory; she was close to tears which glistened on her eyes like dew on a rose petal. Elisabeth put her arm around Grese's shoulder, bolstering for comfort. 'He hit and slapped us all, but he also sexually abused my sister and me when we reached our early teens.'

'Oh Irma, this is awful,' said Elisabeth compassionately. 'Didn't your mother try to stop him?'

'Poor mum couldn't take the violence or the string of affairs he had with other women, so she killed herself when I was only thirteen.' Tear drops began to run down Irma's cheeks, her words now punctuated by sobs, 'I loved my mum and I miss her so much.'

'Oh my God; poor, poor you!' sympathised Elisabeth, squeezing her arm around Irma consolingly. 'I'm suddenly so glad I had a happy childhood.'

The train had reached top speed and the foul stench of Auschwitz began to dissipate into the crispy fresh smell of January. It was too noisy and dark for the other women in the carriage to notice Irma's distress; those who knew and admired Grese would've helped Volkenrath to comfort her. But Irma was tough and tears were an embarrassing nonsense. So, she wiped her eyes and sniffed back the sorrow. 'He also nearly killed my sister, Helena.'

'You mean he tried to kill his own daughter?' questioned Elisabeth.

'It was accidental I suppose.' Irma hesitated to collect her thoughts, 'One of his favourite punishments was to tie us up outside the house and leave us there all night. It didn't matter what time of year it was or what the weather was like. I remember that on one wet winter evening he caught Helena taking some bread without his permission. So, he tied her up outside and left her until morning. As a result, she caught pneumonia and very nearly died.'

'I'm surprised you haven't turned into a serial killer,' said Elisabeth. 'I've read that most of them result from having had an abusive upbringing.'

Irma glanced questioningly sideways at Volkenrath. 'What about our involvement with selections for the gas chamber?' she asked. 'Technically I am an accomplice to a serial killer and so are you.'

'No, we're not; we're just following orders, which happens to be quite different.' She then gave Irma a wicked grin. 'Besides you can't murder a Jew as they're more like rats than people. We're doing them a favour by sending them to hell where they belong.'

This remark amused Grese and consequently began to dissolve the earlier despondent atmosphere. 'Anyway, I left school at fifteen and began training to become a nurse at a SS sanatorium near Hamlin.' Irma looked happy at the thought of these recollections, 'When I saw those hunky SS men, I knew that was what I wanted to become; so as soon as I was old enough, I applied.'

The pair chatted about various subjects through the afternoon and into the night (men and their conquests of them; their time at Auschwitz; what they would like to do after the war) for the entire journey which took eleven hours (including two short toilet-breaks) to a station-stop a few miles south of Berlin. Here Irma (and the other four bound for Ravensbruck) had to disembark with their luggage and wait inside the station building for a pre-arranged troop-transit truck to collect them in the morning. This was because it was considered too dangerous to drive through Berlin city at night due to allied bombing raids, mainly British Bomber Command's revenge for the Luftwaffe's attacks on London. It was considerably warmer here than in Poland and all the women stretched out along separate timber-slatted bench-seats and graciously fell into whispering sleep.

THE AUSWITZ DEATH MARCHES WHICH HAD BEGUN FAR AWAY.

The largest and the most notorious of the death marches took place in the middle of January 1945. On January 12, the Soviet army began its Vistula-Oder Offensive, advancing on occupied Poland. By January 17, orders were given to vacate the Auschwitz concentration camp and its sub-camps. Between the 17th and 21st of this bitterly cold month, the SS began marching approximately fifty-six thousand prisoners out of the Auschwitz camps, most westerly to Loslau 63 kilometres (39 miles) away, but some were sent in a north-westerly direction to Gleiwitz, 55 kilometres (34 miles) away from Auschwitz. Temperatures of −20 °C (−4 °F) and lower were recorded at the time of these marches. Some residents of Upper Silesia tried to help the marching prisoners. Some of the prisoners themselves managed to escape the death marches to freedom. At least three thousand prisoners died on the Gleiwitz route alone. Approximately nine to fifteen thousand prisoners died on these death marches out of Auschwitz's camps, and those who did survive were then put on freight trains and shipped to other camps deeper in German held territory.

From January 17 to 21, the Germans marched approximately 56 thousand prisoners out of Auschwitz and its sub-camps in evacuation columns mostly heading west, through Upper and Lower Silesia. Two days later, they evacuated 2 thousand prisoners by train from the sub-camps in Świętochłowice and Siemianowice. The main evacuation routes led to Wodzisław Śląski and Gliwice, where the many evacuation columns were merged into rail transports. From the sub-camp in Jaworzno, three thousand two hundred prisoners made one of the longest marches—250 kilometres to Gross-Rosen Concentration Camp in Lower Silesia.

The evacuation columns were supposed to consist only of healthy people strong enough to march many score kilometres. In practice, however, sick and enfeebled prisoners also volunteered, since they thought, not without reason, that the Germans would kill those who remained behind. Underage prisoners—Jewish and Polish children—set out on the march along with the adults.

Along all the routes, the escorting SS guards shot both the prisoners who tried to escape and those who were too physically exhausted to keep up with their fellow unfortunates. Thousands of corpses of the prisoners who were shot or who died of fatigue or exposure to the cold lined both the routes where they passed on foot or by train. In Upper Silesia alone, about three thousand evacuated prisoners died. It is estimated that at least nine thousand and more probably fifteen thousand Auschwitz prisoners paid with their lives for the evacuation operation. After the war, the travails of the evacuated prisoners came to be known as the "Death Marches."

One of the few extant Nazi documents referring to the Death Marches is an SS report from March 13, 1945 on the arrival in the Leitmeritz (Litomierzyce) camp in Bohemia of fifty-eight prisoners evacuated from the Auschwitz sub-camp of Hubertushütte, mentioned above. The report states that one hundred and forty-four other prisoners (mostly Jews) died en route.

Massacres of prisoners took place in some of the localities along the evacuation routes. At the Leszczyny/Rzędówka train station near Rybnik on the night of January 21/22, 1945, a train carrying about two thousand five hundred prisoners from Gliwice halted. On the afternoon of January 22, the prisoners were ordered to disembark. Some of them were too exhausted to do so. SS men from the escort and local Nazi police fired machine guns through the open doors of the train cars. The Germans then herded the remaining prisoners westward. After they had marched away, more than three hundred corpses of prisoners, who had been shot or who had died of exhaustion or exposure, were gathered from the grounds of the station and its surroundings.

Many Polish and Czech residents of localities along or near the evacuation route came forward to help the evacuees. For the most part, they gave them water and food, and also sheltered escapees. People in various localities were honoured after the war with the Israel Righteous among the Nations of the World medal for helping escapees survive until liberation.

Documentary material in the collections of the Auschwitz-Birkenau State Museum could also serve as the basis for a precise description of the evacuation of prisoners on the routes from Oświęcim – Gliwice (for prisoners from Monowitz and various other sub-camps) and from the Golleschau sub-camp in Goleszów to Wodzisław Śląski. There is also material on the rail "death transports" through Moravia and Bohemia and some localities in Saxony.

"With the duly vague definition, "Special Squad," the SS referred to the group of prisoners entrusted with running the crematoria. It was their task to maintain order among the new arrivals (often completely unaware of the destiny awaiting them) who were to be sent into the gas chambers, to extract the corpses from the chambers, to pull gold teeth from jaws, to cut women's hair, to sort and classify clothes, shoes, and the content of the luggage, to transport the bodies to the crematoria and oversee the operation of the ovens, to extract and eliminate the ashes. The Special Squad in Auschwitz numbered, depending on the moment, from seven hundred to one thousand active members. These Special Squads did not escape everyone else's fate. On the contrary, the SS exerted the greatest diligence to prevent any man who had been part of it from surviving and telling. Twelve squads succeeded each other for a few months, whereupon it was suppressed, each time with a different trick to head off possible resistance. As its initiation, the next squad burnt the corpses of its predecessors." – Primo Levi

The Blood and the screams

The torture and melancholy depths of misery

The cruelty and the deaths

CHAPTER 7

After convalescing for a few hours at the hospital, Richard was back at home enjoying a glass of whisky. However, he'd told the hospital doctor about the trouble he'd been experiencing with disturbed and infrequent sleep patterns, so the medic had prescribed a course of sleeping pills (Temazepam) which he'd collected from the in-house pharmacy. As Temazepam and alcohol aren't the best of bed-fellows, Richard was determined to limit his drinking habit and only finish half the bottle of whisky before retiring to bed.

The drug worked quickly and he was she again, back in the early winter of 1945. Irma looked out of the windscreen of the bouncing truck as it swerved between bomb-craters and pushed-aside heaps of brick rubble. As Grese was the most senior of the women in the transport she was sat in the warm next to the driver while the others huddled together in the shivering, canvas-canopied rear along with Khan, four other dogs and all the luggage. And Irma was aghast and horrified by the state of bomb destruction which had reduced most of the noble city of Berlin to piles of smashed-up debris; houses, municipal buildings, offices, banks, shops and churches roofless and yawning agape to the frosty elements. Like the spirit escapes from that lethal laceration, it seemed to Irma as if the city had lost its' soul. The shattered buildings that had once stood so arrogantly in ornate gothic terraces, now just smashed-up skeletons of their former glory, like the charred bony remains from the Auschwitz ovens. Mangled floor and roof joists straggled together like broken ribs, splintered furniture and ragged-sodden curtains hanging despondently, dripping with tears as if they were mourners grieving the carnage. Here and there a spire or pinnacle pierced up to the heavens like an omen-warning pointing to the peril expected again from the darkened night sky. Most of the streets had been cleared of bomb debris which had been bulldozed into piles over pavements at the feet of ruins; and despondent, war-weary people (heads sullenly sunk) meandered around between the rubble like those condemned at Auschwitz. The whole city had become a remorse-riddled cemetery of sighs and stricken faces of despair veneered by miserable hopelessness; this was not the Germany the Fuhrer had promised.

Irma spoke to the driver who was a weasel-faced man from the Wehrmacht and who was ridiculously edgy to be in the presence of the SS official sat next to him. 'I've only been to

Berlin once when I was a child. I remember it being such a vibrant and happy city. I can't believe what I'm seeing here.'

'It's terrible isn't it fraulein?' replied the driver nervously, 'So many innocent souls lost.'

Irma was again concentrating on the ruins through the windscreen, 'I remember children dancing around street organs and puppeteers on the pavement; bright lights and gaiety.'

'It'll be a long time before we see that again, fraulein,' replied the driver morosely.

As they neared the northern limits of the city the truck began to slow, as up-ahead was a check-point. The lorry stopped at the barrier and two Wehrmacht guards approached one to either side of the vehicle. The driver began to wind-down his window, and, as he did so, said to Irma, 'They will want to check your ID card; I hope you have it on you.'

'Of course,' replied Grese reaching into the inside pocket of her jacket. 'I never go anywhere without it.' When the other guard reached her side of the truck she wound-down the window and instantly recognised those eyes peeping-out from the shadow cast by the brim of his tin helmet. 'Josef?' she questioned, astonished.

'Irma please get out of the truck.' She did as he asked, and Mengele took her across the street, away from curious ears. 'I know we've had our differences recently,' he said with an urgent intonation, 'But I want to help you.'

'What the hell do you mean?' Grese questioned, her beautiful face screwed with curiosity.

'To get you out of the SS like I've managed to do.'

'Why would I want to leave the SS?' she asked.

'Because Germany will lose this war, and quite soon.' He sighed despairingly. 'You see the Allied forces are on all fronts and are quickly gaining ground.' He looked at her pleadingly, 'Can you imagine what will happen when they discover the concentration camps and catch those who worked in them?'

'No and why should I care? I've done nothing wrong and only followed orders,' Grese replied casually.

Mengele looked at her with awful knowledge. 'I have it on good authority that all those involved in the Final Solution will be tried for crimes against humanity.'

'Well, surely going to court is better than being shot for desertion?'

Mengele shook his head with frustration. 'Look you won't be deserting if you join the Wehrmacht; or you could simply pose as a civilian. I'm leaving Germany in a couple of days to join my wife in South America; you could come with me. I know someone who can issue you with a new identity and eradicate your history within the SS; then you can't be taken to court for war crimes.'

Irma thought for a moment before she replied. 'I know exactly what you want from me,' she said sharply. 'Well, you can get that from your bloody wife from now on as I'm in love with Franz.' She glowered at him spitefully. 'Goodbye Josef,' she said bleakly, before turning and heading back to the lorry.

*

Although it was only a little under one hundred miles (one hundred and sixty-one kilometres) from the railway station to Ravensbruck, it took them almost six hours to get there, and half of that time was spent trying to negotiate a route through Berlin; many times the truck had turned around or reversed due to streets being blocked by bomb debris. And Irma knew when they were close to their destination as her sense-of-smell was, once again, affronted by that familiar awful odour, the unmistakeable stench of death.

Unlike Auschwitz, which had been adapted from former Polish soldier's barracks, Ravensbruck had been built from new and to order and formed a camp which constantly evolved into an ever-more efficient killing machine, comprising of prison blocks, crematoria and a gas chamber. Apart from the death and body-disposal buildings, the prisoner's barrack dormitory blocks replicated each other; long pre-fabricated rectangular structures in two rows with a courtyard in-between. Appropriately, the buildings aligned with the precise and awful symmetry of a war-grave cemetery and the whole area was enclosed by a thirteen foot (four metres) high red-brick wall atop of which was a lethal inward-curling, electric barb-wire fence fixed to four foot long, banana-shaped metal prongs. Outside of this impenetrable boundary were the SS quarters and the camp commander's villa, a ruthless and despotic SS officer who went by the name of Fritz Suhren.

Ravensbruck had developed from its inception and now contained fourteen prison barracks, two hospital blocks, a wooden kitchen and a shower hut; nine more barracks for the four thousand female slave-labourer prisoners who toiled for eleven hours daily in several Siemens Engineering factories that surrounded the camp; there were four more sparsely populated and well-furnished blocks allocated to the Siemens-employed permanent staff. Over the entire site, two barracks served as a prisoners' sickbay (only used by essential workers), two more served as warehouses, one served as a penal block and one more functioned as an over-night punishment lock-up for errant or paralytic SS guards. The twelve remaining barracks served as the prisoners' housing, in which prisoners slept in three rows of triple-tiered wooden bunks.

Ravensbruck was almost exclusively a woman's camp of Jews, Gypsies, Poles, a few Russians and some political prisoners; however, there was a very small men's camp, the occupants of which were used as labour to maintain the gas chamber and crematoria. The camp was designed to take six thousand prisoners but by this late stage of the war it contained around thirty thousand, all crammed shoulder to shoulder in their quarters like sardines. But as inmates perished in these appalling, suffocating conditions their dwindling numbers were not replaced as those coming in on death marches and trains were simply sent straight to their miserable demise, either by a mass firing squad or into the gas chamber which struggled to cope with the heinous demand. With the threat of the allies advancing, the Nazi killing machine had become efficiently ruthless, like fighting a fire with petrol.

Of course, Irma Grese was familiar with Ravensbruck as she'd undergone Aufseherin training at the camp just a couple of years beforehand; but it was much busier now with several new buildings having been erected. It had turned into a mucky day, the atmosphere swimming with a foggy drizzle (scotch-mist we call it in the UK) but, as the camp's location was fifty-six miles (ninety kilometres) north of Berlin, the damp-whirling air was noticeably warmer than at Auschwitz. Irma and the other female guards, struggling with luggage and trying to control excited bouncy dogs, were met at the camp's entrance with a happy, welcoming smile from the Commandant Fritz Suhren who remembered the blonde belle's exceptional beauty.

'Hello my dear Iggy,' he said grinning, fat with civility and smarmy charm. 'My goodness! You're even more beautiful than I remember,' he added, ogling her feminine curves lecherously, 'And may I say how delighted I am to have you back here.' Then his eyes travelled around the rest of the group, 'Welcome ladies to Ravensbruck,' then admiringly back to Irma. 'Let me take those,' he said seizing the handles of her suitcases, 'Now come on, let's get out of this filthy weather.'

The group of women followed the Commandant through the main gates, which were promptly fastened shut behind them, and onto a tarmac courtyard glistening with moisture, glossy like black satin. Although the area was writhing with the unrelenting toils of the prisoners, scuttling here and there like headless chickens, to one sparsely populated side of the square stood a group of four SS guards surrounding three glamorously dressed young women (obviously not ordinary prisoners) who wobbled precariously a couple of feet above the ground, each balancing on a three-legged stool, the nooses ensnaring their necks suspended from the bar of the gallows above. Because of their stylish appearance, Irma was intrigued. So, she casually asked Suhren who they were.

'British spies, my dear,' he told her. 'Girls that were captured in Berlin and who once worked for the allied Special Operations Executive.'

As Grese and the others watched the scene with dreadful intrigue, the guards kicked the stools away from under the women and the three of them swung from their necks a few inches above the ground, writhing helplessly like out-of-the-river fish struggling on the angler's line, until each body reluctantly conceded to its' fate and, with a final death-twitch, a heroine's life grudgingly drained away; with it memories of the past, the here-and-now of the present and hopes for the future were savagely expunged; just dangling corpses swinging mournfully from the last throes of life and casting ghostly shadows that spun sombrely on the ground; the inert shade of death. And the guards laughed raucously as murder amongst the savage ranks of the SS was recreation, violence which was never accused and always pardoned.

Richard was sat on the settee in Tony Ludlow's therapy room talking to the doctor who was seated opposite him and listening intently to what he had to say. 'Despite the fact I've been prescribed sleeping pills, I had another terrible dream last night.' The deacon emitted a deep sigh of remorse, 'I watched three women being hung from gallows. It was very vivid almost as if I were actually there.'

'My goodness,' said Ludlow, his tone and manner consoling. 'What else can you tell me about your nightmare?'

'That's the problem; most of it's a blur and I just seem to remember the horrible bits.'

Ludlow looked thoughtful and scratched his head indicatively. 'I think these dreams must be sparked-off by your dreadful upbringing.'

Richard shook his head negatively. 'That might have something to do with it, but I can't see the connection because those old dreams about my father have been replaced by these horrible new ones.'

'Well, that's for me to establish,' said the psychiatrist assuredly. 'But what makes you so hesitant about the connection to your childhood?'

Richard wavered for a moment because his thoughts and personal understanding of his plight seemed ludicrously make-believe and nonsense. Nevertheless, Ludlow was there to help so he'd better spill the beans and explain. He shook his head again, 'You won't believe this but I think my dreams are about some kind of prison camp back in either World War One or World War Two.'

Ludlow didn't look surprised. 'That would explain the Nazi ideologies you rant about when having a brain seizure.' He paused momentarily for thought, 'Have you seen the movie Schindler's List?'

'I've heard of it but it's not something I'd want to watch.'

The psychiatrist noticed that Richard suddenly looked bemused and a little troubled. 'Are you alright?' he asked, concerned.

So, the young deacon explained. 'Even as a small child I knew I wanted to become a priest someday and so, as a devout Christian, I've studied our Saviour's teachings about love and peace and know very little about wars and hatred.' He looked at the doctor quizzically, 'So how is it possible that I dream about it so vividly?'

'I don't know,' replied Ludlow. 'But what you've just said has given me an idea; please come with me into my study.'

Inside the office, the doctor pulled up a chair and placed it beside his own behind a desk. He then switched on a computer and gestured for Richard to sit alongside him. When the two men were sat together, Ludlow used the mouse to point the computer's cursor at the Google window. Once the internet screen flashed up, he typed "concentration camps" into the search bar recalling Richard's earlier reference to prison camps and cleverly tying that to his patient's dream-pattern and in-trance outbursts.

As soon as the appropriate page sparked on the screen, Richard pointed at a colour photograph of a low but long, single-storey red-brick building under a terracotta-tile pitched roof; in the middle of this structure was a narrow, three-storey, pinnacle-topped tower enclosing an arch through which tunnelled a railway track. Suddenly his innocence was affronted and slapped by unexpected and uninvited guilt. 'I don't understand why, but I vaguely recognise that place and yet I've never been there or seen a picture of it before.'

The doctor knew that it was a photo of the train entrance to the notorious Auschwitz death camp; however, he didn't let on this knowledge and simply said to his patient, 'That's very interesting and this might very well help me with my research into your case.'

Tony Ludlow switched off the computer.

*

Back at home Richard was intrigued as a result of his session with Ludlow so flipped open his laptop and repeated the Google search the doctor had made earlier. On the same page that the psychiatrist had found he clicked the cursor on the photo of the red-brick building....Auschwitz Concentration Camp...He'd heard of that before, something to do with Nazi Germany killing Jews in World War Two. Why did they want to kill Jews? Jesus Christ the Messiah was Jewish; surely the Germans had religion back then? So why would they want to murder the race from which the Saviour originated? Richard thought deeply, throwing his memory back to the many wise words he'd learnt in Bible classes and other religious teachings. There was of course the obvious from the Ten Commandments (number 5 – Thou shall not kill!) but then some of the words from Psalm eighty-three flashed into his reasoning:

"O God, do not remain silent; do not turn a deaf ear, do not stand aloof, O God. See how your enemies growl, how your foes rear their heads. With cunning they conspire against your people; they plot against those you cherish. "Come," they say, "let us destroy them as a nation, so that Israel's name is remembered no more." With one mind they plot together; they form an alliance against you."

Could the words in this psalm be one of the reasons? Had the Nazis misinterpreted the meaning or was it simply racial hatred? The psalm was a plea from Israel asking God to protect its people from their enemies, something he certainly failed to do at Auschwitz. Or did God ignore his son's plea for *clemency on the cross and plot an ultimate holocaust-revenge against Christ's Jewish murderers - the Sanhedrin (Council if Judges) who'd demanded his execution by their Roman potentates?

* *"Father, forgive them; for they know not what they do."*

Puzzled by his thoughts, the young curate was now in two minds; on the one hand he wanted to deepen his research into Auschwitz, on the other he was frightened by what he might discover. Aware of his religious convictions and timid sensibilities, the prospect of further study into the subject was like meat to the mouth of the vegan. His finger hovered over the laptop's mouse, ready to click on a blue-highlighted link on the page...dare he? To do so would be against his better-judgement; but his curiosity was at a peak. What if the link led to pictures he recognised; rooms he'd been in but hadn't? People he knew but didn't? Dutch-courage was needed, so he poured himself a large glass of whisky, glugged it back in two enormous mouthfuls, and then determinedly hit the button. The page flashed-up with colour photos of more red-brick buildings and rows of barbed-wire fences; sepia-coloured ones of sad-faced and resigned-to-fate people (men, women and children) struggling forlornly on a railway platform while others disembarked from windowless train carriages; all done under the cruel-faced attention of soldiers with dogs. To Richard's fragile feelings the black and white photos were very disturbing; but luckily there was nothing he recognised so he folded down the laptop's lid, had a couple more glasses of whisky, a sleeping pill then retired to bed.

*

It was the end of Irma Grese's first day back at Ravensbruck and the drizzle had been shooed away by a climatic high. She had just enjoyed a delicious evening meal, compliments of the Commandant and his wife and held in the privacy of their luxurious villa. She and Suhren were now outside drinking schnapps while chatting idly together; they sat next to each other in a bubble of platonic intimacy (Irma scrunched-up with her knees beneath her chin), swinging peacefully on a bench-seat attached by ropes to the ceiling of a timber veranda which abutted the front of his home. The clear winter sky was studded with stars, like diamonds scattered over a face of coal and Irma loved the romance of star-gazing especially when her thoughts were fuzzed by mind-tickling alcohol. She looked up at the sky lazily and said to Fritz, 'Did you know that the furthest star you can see with a naked eye is over sixteen thousand light years away?'

'No, I didn't' replied Suhren, switching his attention from the flickering lights illuminating Ravensbruck, up to the heavens above. 'How do you know?' he asked.

'Because I'm clever,' replied Irma, giggling mischievously as a magpie. 'But I must admit I don't know how they worked it out.'

'With science and maths, I expect.'

'But that simply doesn't make sense,' said Grese, eyes-up and still admiring the star-speckled night-sky.

'Why not?' questioned Fritz, 'They're clever people these mathematicians and astrologers. They use special mathematical formulas; x and y and so forth.'

'Algebra, you mean? I hated that at school.'

'And logarithms Iggy.'

'I hated that too,' spat Irma. 'But for any of these distance calculations surely you have to have scale?'

'You mean to calculate distance you'd need a measurement of some sort?' asked Fritz, thoughtfully.

'Exactly,' said Irma. 'And the shortest distance between two objects is a straight line.'

'What's your point?' quizzed Suhren.

'My point is this. If someone invented a measuring-stick device that was able to travel at the speed of light and pointed it at that remote star sixteen thousand million light years away, surely they'd have to wait thirty-two thousand million light years to get the answer?'

Fritz exploded with laughter, and then added, 'Yes, I take your point.'

Irma looked thoughtful again. 'You know the Americans are often seeing spaceships?'

'Yes, there were several reports of sightings before the war.'

'Well, if some of those stars out there support a solar system like ours, and if my measurement theory is correct, those little green men might be closer than we think!'

Suhren squirmed with more laughter.

Grese pulled her gaze from the stars and focused her thoughts on the subject that niggled her intellect. She gave Fritz a squint of concern, 'Changing the subject, do you think we're about to lose this war?'

Suhren answered immediately. 'I'm quite sure Adolf Hitler won't permit that to happen. He's a shrewd man and is bound to have something up his sleeve.

*

"Close your eyes and listen. Listen to the silent screams of terrified mothers, the prayers of anguished old men and women. Listen to the tears of children. Jewish children; a beautiful little girl among them with golden hair whose vulnerable tenderness has never left me. Look and listen as they walk towards dark flames so gigantic that the planet itself seemed in danger."- Elie Wiesel.

CHAPTER 8

The following day was clear and chilly, but Irma didn't notice the cold as her body was still acclimatised to the bitter temperatures she'd had to endure at Auschwitz. This was her first official duty-day back at Ravensbruck and she'd been assigned as lead-charge to four prison barrack-blocks; as she walked defiantly towards them her intrigue was attracted by a line of SS guards standing in front of a huge pit dug into the ground in a corner of the compound. At first, she couldn't see the purpose of the hole but her curiosity was magnetised and she approached to find out. She sneaked up behind the male guards and stood unseen behind them, then peered down from a gap in-between their figures; down there, into the hollowed depth of the pit, were hundreds of naked, bone-tight corpses, all tangled together in a macabre tapestry of lifeless shrunken limbs and agape death-gawps. But Grese's eyes were accustomed to such gruesome sights as she watched a cart-full of more skeletal carcasses being pushed by four struggling-with-the-weight female prisoners towards the pit.

When the cart reached the pit-side the four women tried to push its' handles up, to tip the corpses into the abyss of death; but they were simply too weak, tired and malnourished to manage. So, one of the guards lifted his rifle and aimed it threatingly at the women.

Irma stepped in feeling defiantly feminist, 'Don't shoot them, I'll give them a hand.'

All the men spun their attention at her. As they'd never laid eyes on her before, she could tell from the look on their faces that they were stunned by her beauty; it was that display of admiring eyes and ingratiating smiles she was becoming accustomed to, something that tingled her self-esteem and flattered her ego. So, Irma went round to the women struggling with the cart as did two of her new admirers and helped to tip the cart. The corpses flopped out; flailing like rag-dolls into the tangle of the others in the pit; and those which landed on their backs stared upwards with the white-eyed, horror-stricken agony of a forced, untimely and uninvited death.

*

Richard's eyes snapped open with the horror of this haunting reverie and those pure-white death-eyes protruding from a torn and sullied face that yawned toothlessly from its' cry of final despair; however, his body was riddled with fatigue from the cocktail of whisky and Temazepam. He glanced across at the alarm clock-9.36am; he'd better get his skates on as he had another appointment with Ludlow at eleven. So, he rose from bed lethargically and, sleepy-eyed, left his bedroom for a cold drink to relieve the gritty, hangover dryness that choked his throat. As he approached the fridge to pour himself a wake-up glass of milk he noticed something very disturbing. Richard had magnetic plastic letters attached to the fridge door which he used for shopping-list reminders; someone or something had used these to form the following words which looked to be in German: "EIN VOLK, EIN REICH, EIN FUHRER." Richard immediately opened his laptop for the translation which was: "ONE PEOPLE, ONE NATION, ONE LEADER.' He stared at the words disbelievingly; was he still asleep and dreaming again? Or maybe his recent computer search for Auschwitz had acted like an Ouija board and subpoenaed some evil Nazi demon? But grudgingly he realised it had most likely been himself from a misguided sleep-walk related to his turbulent dreams.

Richard Pope arrived almost ten minutes late at the Psychiatry Practise for his therapy session with Tony Ludlow; however, the psychiatrist welcomed him with his usual friendly gusto and sucked him into the therapy room. Richard sat where he had before but Ludlow paced back and forth, hand-to-chin, in front of him (from a bookcase then crossing the room to a standing lamp-then back again and so on). The doctor was pondering, his shiny bald head almost throbbing with thoughts; it was the corollary movements and demeanour of a man about to share a revelation which he then proceeded to do, stopping his marched parade and turning to address his client.

'After we finished the session yesterday, I spent all afternoon and evening researching your case,' he sharpened his focus on Richard, 'And I've found five cases in the last ten years that showed similar symptoms to yours.'

'That's good,' said Richard, 'So do you know how to treat me?'

'It's not that simple, I'm afraid,' replied Ludlow cautiously. 'If I thought you were suffering from a schizophrenic disorder or a psychotic break then that'd be fairly easy to deal with and treat.'

'Well, it has to be something like that as these vivid dreams have only occurred since they operated on my brain.'

The doctor walked around his chair and sat opposite his client as he had on their previous meeting. 'One of these five cases I mentioned earlier was studied by a very eminent American psychologist and author called Professor Abraham Benowitz,' Ludlow hesitated as if gathering thoughts, 'So I looked him up on the web and took the liberty to phone him.'

'Was he able to help you?' asked the young deacon.

'Yes, he was, in theory anyway...It's a good thing you're sitting down.' The doctor's client screwed his brow with intrigue, 'Let me ask you an odd question; odd because it doesn't seem related.'

'I'm all ears Mr Ludlow,' said Richard.

'Okay then...Do you believe in reincarnation?'

Richard appeared a little surprised by the question. 'Of course, I do,' he replied positively. 'As a Christian and member of the Church of England we believe that our Saviour Jesus Christ rose from the dead as we all are destined to do.'

'Yes of course,' realising the error (almost stupidity) of his earlier question. 'Did you know that you passed away after your accident?'

'Yes, the doctor at the hospital told me I was very lucky and that a passing ambulance crew with a defibrillator managed to re-start my heart.'

Ludlow nodded in acknowledgement. 'Well, Benowitz told me of a possible explanation based on the case study of one of his patients. He has a theory that sometimes when the spirit leaves the body it can regress in time to a former incarnation.'

Richard looked utterly captivated by Ludlow's explanation. 'You mean, because I died, I'm the reincarnation of someone else who's dead?'

'That's basically Benowitz' theory and it's possible that he might be right.'

'But who?' asked Richard urgently, 'A priest at Auschwitz?'

'That we don't know; but judging by your Nazi orientated in-trance outbursts I very much doubt it's a priest.'

The deacon emitted a disgruntled sigh. 'If this is the case, how am I going to find out who I once was and how do I put a stop to the nightmares?'

'I'm not sure,' replied Ludlow limply. 'Benowitz was very busy when I phoned him so I had to cut my call short. However, he gave me his home telephone number and told me to phone him at the weekend. One thing that he did suggest is that you should try to remember your dream as soon as you wake up, that way it'll hopefully lodge in your memory.'

'Okay, I'll do that next time. However, there's something I haven't told you yet,' said Richard. He continued cautiously, 'When I went to my fridge this morning the words ONE PEOPLE, ONE NATION, ONE LEADER were written in German on the door using the magnetic letters I've stuck on it. I think I must've done it in my sleep.'

The doctor looked thoughtful. 'I assume you don't know how to speak German?'

'Not a word.'

'How strange; perhaps the words on your fridge door will give us some clues and I'll make sure I speak to Benowitz again this weekend.'

With that Ludlow ended the session early because he was tired with the extra-to-curriculum work he'd put in on the behalf of the young apprentice priest.

*

1945 again and February had just tumbled into March. Outside of the fences of the Ravensbruck camp, trees and shrubs were awakening from their winter hibernation and birds sang cheerily from gnarled boughs; buds were starting to burst lime-green and daffodils pushed reluctantly up through the cold and soggy mire. But inside the camp, death-dark clouds of bone-meal pervaded the gloomy atmosphere, belching out from the chimneys of the crematorium and from several pits where SS guards soused corpses in petrol or diesel and set them ablaze. No bird song here, just the misery of the wretched and agony of the damned in an infinite and unremitting tragedy.

Irma Grese was outside in the courtyard, stood to abrupt attention within a line of ten other female guards who were being addressed by a medical officer Gruppenfuhrer (two-star Lieutenant) Karl Gebhardt who was a short, stout and unpleasant looking man in his late forties.

'Do any of you dear ladies have any medical experience,' he asked unctuously. Irma stood forward from the line and raised her arm. The Lieutenant approached her. Gebhardt had a tight face, one that couldn't easily smile, and when he tried to force one, he looked even uglier than normal. 'How much involvement did you have, my dear?'

Irma answered his question. 'I trained as a nurse for a couple of years before joining the Schutzstaffel.'

'I'm after an assistant. Would you like to help me, my dear?'

Grese thought quickly, the answer instant; helping him would be interesting and might exclude her from some of the more onerous chores such as roll calls in the rain. 'Yes, I'd like that very much,' she happily agreed.

'Excellent, my dear.' He spread his smile grotesquely, 'By the way, what is your name?'

'Irma Grese, Sir; but colleagues call me Iggy,' she replied.

'Very good Iggy, meet me in the medical centre after lunch.' He then stood back from Irma and addressed the others in the rank of women guards, 'Thank you ladies, you're all dismissed.'

*

It was a few minutes after two o'clock that Irma Grese entered the medical centre at Ravensbruck. It was a hygienically clean room that smelt of sweet/sour antiseptic. It was also uncluttered with three metal operating tables in the middle overlooked by medical cabinets (some glazed, some not) attached floor-to-ceiling on three of the four walls, the fourth just two doors and some windows through which hazy-light, clouded by smoke from the crematorium, struggled inward. To oust the gloom, bright lights shone ebulliently down from above the operating tables, two of which were occupied by the face-down anaesthetised naked bodies of two women, torsos of which sunk and rose with reluctant life.

Then Karl Gebhardt came up into the room from a cellar below; he was wearing a white unbuttoned lab-coat and rubber gloves. At once he noticed Irma standing there looking slightly bemused. 'Hello my dear Iggy,' he said, trying but failing to sound ingratiating. He approached one of the women on the operating table, 'Come over here, my dear,' he said across the room to Grese. She did as asked, and Gebhardt handed her a large syringe. 'I want you to use this to draw blood away from the incision I'm about to make on the woman's lower leg,' he explained.

Hunched over his victim like Quasimodo, Gebhardt then tied a tourniquet tightly above the woman's knee and her lower limb began to fade in colour as the blood-rush slowed. He looked up at Irma again, 'I've got to be extremely careful where I cut because there are both the Popliteal and Peroneal arteries in there,' he said pointing at the woman's calf muscles. 'There's also the Achilles tendon I'd like to avoid if possible.'

Irma looked puzzled. 'Why are you operating on this woman's leg?' she asked. 'There doesn't appear to be anything wrong with it.'

'I want to graft some bone from her fibula onto that of the other woman asleep behind you and vice versa.' The smiley grimace was gone, Gebhardt looked lost in thought. 'It's a procedure I've attempted several times before but with very limited success. I think I may now have perfected a method using a new form of sterilisation.'

'But for what reason?' Irma questioned.

'Because I'm told the war is closing in and the fighting will get worse. If I can conceive a method to repair shattered bones that may help some of our boys involved in the conflict to fight on.' He then re-concentrated on his target, picked up a scalpel and plunged it into his victim's calf, drawing the full depth of the blade down the limb like a hot knife through butter.

Irma Grese began to suck the leaking flow of blood with the syringe.

"They took those legs that so loved movement and dancing, and removed a large section of bone from them. Then, for good measure, they injected them with bacteria. She lay there, butchered, her legs in plaster - still trying to smile." – Wanda Poltawska

The first group of experiments (ended in 1943) was designed to test the effectiveness of Sulfanilamide drugs using several methods designed to cause severe infections. The description of the procedures was provided by Doctor Fritz Fischer, later a defendant at Nuremberg. A surgical incision on the outside of the lower leg, the wound was filled with bacteria and sewn up. In the course of experiments, progressively more virulent bacteria were used; such as streptococcus, gangrene, and tetanus; wood shavings and glass were added to the mix and blood circulation was interrupted by tying off blood vessels at both ends of the wound to create a condition similar to that of a battlefield.

Bone Operations (under anaesthetic to stop them wriggling): Only women had to endure these cruel experiments:

The operations, during which bones were broken, lasted up to three hours, during which time the shin bones of both legs were exposed then broken with hammers on the operating table. Then the bones were set with the aid of clamps (sometimes without them) and the wounds were crudely sewn shut; then these severely injured (inexpertly hacked) limbs were cocooned within plaster-casts. After a few days (before the wounds had healed) the plaster-cast was taken off and the broken extremities were left to heal without the protection of any form of dressing. If the patient (better word VICTIM) disliked the indignity of a bed-pan and attempted to walk to the toilet, both legs would snap under her weight resulting in the poor woman being shot in the head where she lay. Other heinous experiments involved bone grafts from one patient to another where a square bone splinter was removed from the bone (usually in both shins and usually in two places) and implanted into another victim's leg

Muscle Operations: (under anaesthetic)

During these operations, pieces of muscle were removed from the lower extremities, both from the thigh and shin. The victims were operated on several times, removing larger and larger pieces of muscle the second and third times, causing larger and larger holes and greater weakness of the affected areas. It was a flesh-grafting experiment where the muscle from a recently deceased gas-chamber victim would be grafted into an exactly shaped incision-wound (cut-out) on the living recipient. Because of lack of success (flesh-grafts being rejected by the immune system of the recipient's body,) this practise was largely ceased in 1943 as an ineffectual waste-of-time and waste of valuable resources.

"I swore never to be silent whenever and wherever human beings endure suffering and humiliation. We must take sides. Neutrality helps the oppressor, never the victim. Silence encourages the tormentor, never the tormented." – Elie Wiesel

*

It was the Monday after the last cut-short session with the psychiatrist and Richard was boxed out of bed and landed on his hands and knees; but it was an unfair contest to spar against three opponents, the nightmare, a sleeping pill and alcohol. However, the Lennox Lewis punch had been that awful dream about the deep incision into that young woman's leg. As he'd just woken up, he took Ludlow's recent advice and tried to recall the reverie, slotting the prominent parts into his troubled memory; but who or what was Iggy? He struggled to get to his feet, haggard by the dregs of sleep, then wobbled his way to the fridge for that cool glass of milk to ease the whisky-induced grittiness that stifled and sucked his mouth and throat. Before he swung open the fridge door, he noticed that the magnetic plastic letters stuck to it had been moved again and now formed a sentence in German which read "MEIN EHRE HEISST TREUE." Richard opened the fridge-door, gulped back milk straight from the carton then opened his laptop to search for the translation. He was deeply shocked by what he discovered; he'd heard of a German regiment in World War Two known as the SS, a military unit notorious for their wickedness. The translation of the fridge-magnet letters read "MY HONOUR IS CALLED LOYALTY" which (the browser informed him) just happened to be the motto of this evil regiment.

Richard was a few minutes late for his appointment with Tony Ludlow but the doctor was as welcoming as ever. They sat opposite each other as before in the therapy room and Richard related his most recent dream to the psychiatrist, the best that he could remember it; this was about that awful experimental operation his sub-conscious had witnessed and the fact that someone had referred to him as Iggy. So, they went into Ludlow's office and tried another computer search – Iggy and the holocaust – then – Iggy at Auschwitz – but found no clues to the identity of this mysterious individual.

So, they settled back into the therapy room and Tony Ludlow began to reveal his weekend telephone conversation with the American psychologist Abraham Benowitz. 'He told me that he had a very similar case to yours,' said the doctor, focusing his full attention on Richard, 'And he referred to the phenomenon as pre-incarnation.'

'So, you think this may be what I'm experiencing?' asked the young deacon.

'It's possible,' said Ludlow, dryly. 'Now allow me to explain about the Benowitz' case. His client was an African American and, like you, a man of God, a pastor I think he said. Anyway, he died on the operating table while undergoing a heart-bypass and, like you, was resuscitated. After this he began to have terrible nightmares similar to those you experience.'

'This is interesting,' said Richard. 'Did Benowitz cure him of the nightmares and what were they about?'

'He dreamt of being a serial-killer who murdered men, women and children in the late 1800's and early twentieth century.' Ludlow scratched his chin in thought, 'Benowitz explained to me that this was strange because his patient was a good and God-fearing man and murderous and malicious thoughts had never crossed his mind before.'

'But was he cured?'

'Not to start with, but this is where it gets interesting. This murderer was taken to court for allegedly poisoning a man. It was at the preliminary hearing that the judge mentioned the murderers' name; the Pastor remembered the dream and the name stated at the trial and so they were able to research into the killer.' Ludlow paused unnecessarily to deliver the surprising revelation.

Richard was on the edge of his seat. 'Go on...' he urged, 'I'm all ears.'

'Well, it's intriguing; as it turned out that the killer was a white woman called Belle Gunness.'

For a brief moment Richard's intrigued gawp looked wide enough to swallow a football. Once the doctor's words had settled in his reasoning, he asked, 'So when they found out who the Pastor was dreaming about, did the nightmares stop?'

'Not to start with but Belle Gunness died before the second hearing and that's when the nightmares ceased.'

'Do you think Iggy is also a woman? And does that mean I've got to wait until he or she dies in my pre-incarnated life before I stop having these horrid dreams?' asked the young man dispiritedly. 'That might be years away.'

'Describing what you have about your dreams, I doubt they involve a woman; it just seems too cruel for the fairer sex,' said Ludlow sagely. 'As for the other point you raise, I'm quite certain Iggy isn't a serial-killer like Gunness so I expect your nightmares will finish along with the end of the war that raged during the period you're dreaming about.'

'Well, I hope you're right,' sighed the young deacon. 'I'm sure whoever it is in my dreams is a member of a brigade called the SS.'

'That vicious gang of bullies,' spat the doctor. 'However, that makes sense as they were the force behind the holocaust which we think you're dreaming about. But how do you know?'

'Fridge magnets again; this morning they spelt out MY HONOUR IS CALLED LOYALTY in German and on my computer's translation I discovered it was the slogan the SS used.'

Ludlow: 'I think I ought to try and stop this sleep-walking as it could be dangerous. Although I can prescribe medicines, I think you should check with the surgeon who operated on you for his advice. Try and see him this afternoon and tell him I recommend a short course of Zimovane to try and get an untroubled sleep-pattern established.'

*

Belle Gunness was an American serial killer known as "The Black Widow". Born in Selbu, Norway, in 1859, Gunness longed to move to the United States and so immigrated to America in 1881. She immediately began money-making schemes and used cunning and deception to make a small fortune through insurance fraud. She also left a trail of nearly 40 bodies in her wake.

From an outsider's perspective, it seemed like a never-ending spell of disasters befell the unfortunate Gunness, much more than would normally be expected. People who knew her felt sorry for this pitiable but likeable frail woman struck by one tragedy after another. But all of the "accidents" were carefully and brutally orchestrated by Gunness so she could make money from insurance claims.

She began to kill around 1893 after she married her first husband, Mads Sorenson. They opened up a store together and had four children and one foster child.

First, the couple's business burned down. Next, two of her children abruptly died from acute colitis. Acute colitis and strychnine poisoning share similar symptoms. However due to the infancy of medical procedures (autopsy and pathology investigations) these incidents were seen as unfortunate coincidences and did not raise any alarm bells.

The day following the deaths of her children her husband died under suspicious circumstances. She murdered him for the worth of valuable life insurance. Although suspicions were raised it couldn't be proved that he hadn't died of natural causes and so monies were paid to her from two policies which he held.

With the proceeds from this murderous scheming, Gunness then moved her family to La Porte, Indiana and bought a 42-acre farm. It wasn't long before she burned it to the ground in order to collect more insurance monies. Rather than rebuilding the farm she converted a barn in the grounds into living accommodation thus saving a fortune.

She eventually re-married to Peter Gunness who added two daughters, from his previous marriage, to the household. When one child died under mysterious circumstances, Peter grew suspicious and sent his eldest daughter to stay with relatives. This ended up being the correct decision as she was the only child to survive Bella's killing campaign.

Shortly after this, Peter himself was killed when a meat grinder allegedly fell on his head in the kitchen. Gunness collected his life insurance policy and later gave birth to their son.

Now a professional serial killer, Bella thought of another effective and less noticeable way to earn blood-money. She took out newspaper advertisements asking for male companionship. Several wealthy men visited her farm with money bulging in their pockets; none left it alive.

According to Jack Rosewood, author of "Hell's Princess: The Mystery of Belle Gunness, Butcher of Men", Gunness was brutal in her treatment of her victims' bodies as she often chopped them up like farm animals and then buried these grisly remains in her backyard.

In 1908, Gunness' luck seemed to run out. Her farmhouse again burned to the ground, and the bodies of her remaining three children were found in the wreckage alongside a headless body which the police believed belonged to Gunness herself.

Coincidentally, the brother of one of Bella's victims had come to town to investigate his sibling's disappearance, and he urged police to investigate the burned farm's grounds. On searching the property, authorities found the bodies of forty men and children.

Because the police thought the headless woman was the corpse of Gunness, her new lover, Ray Lamphere, was arrested for murder and arson. However, there was no evidence to support this and he was able to give a concrete alibi so was eventually cleared of the charge. Nonetheless, his alibi revealed that he was guilty of other crimes in the area and was sent to gaol. Years later, on his death-bed in prison, Lamphere revealed the truth, that Bella Gunness was a serial killer. He confessed that she burned her own house down and that the headless body the authorities had believed to be hers belonged to another of her victims.

Gunness was never found, and her death has never been confirmed. However, a woman in California (who was around Bella's age) died in 1931 while awaiting trial for poisoning a man. In her possession were photos of three children who resembled those who'd once belonged to Bella Gunness.

CHAPTER 9

Richard didn't go to the hospital for advice about Zimovane because he was frightened that this powerful new drug might prevent him from waking from a nightmare, thus witnessing an entire episode of some holocaust atrocity without being able to escape by awakening; that was something he must prevent at all costs. It was a beautiful afternoon in the middle of April 2012 and the young deacon considered it was time for spiritual reflection, the type that verges on meditation. There was only one place where he felt completely at ease, only one place that evoked the peaceful environment required for deep contemplation and prayer; that was to be with God in his church. Now the bishop had asked him to keep from entering the building until his mental health had improved and his case was assured and signed-off by the psychiatrist. Of course, the bishop was too busy with business appertaining to his diocese to phone Doctor Ludlow for updates about his patient's wellbeing, so knew nothing about the mind-troubles the young man was still experiencing and the dreadful nightmares about Iggy. And Richard had missed the important Easter services he loved to attend because of the bishop's softly-softly demand; but the prelate's injunction had only referred to the church itself and hadn't mentioned the grounds in which it stood. Richard took it as read as to the extent of the no-go area (to include the place-of-worship and its' grounds) but felt a little defiant just as his Lord Jesus had been with the money-changers in the temple.

"And making a whip of cords, he drove them all out of the temple, with the sheep and oxen. And poured out the coins of the money-changers and overturned their tables. And he told those who sold the pigeons, 'Take these things away; do not make my Father's house a place of trade.'"

So, the taxi dropped him off at the church where he proceeded through the churchyard, which trilled with jaunty birdsong, over the grassy cemetery (via a respectful slalom of headstones) to a bench beneath the ancient, spikey-black-boughs of a yew tree. Here Richard sat all alone, half in shade and half in sunshine that fizzed with midges and which bathed him soothingly in its vivaciously convivial warmth. He breathed-in the thought-invoking peacefulness then cupped the palms of his hands over his eyes (elbows on knees) and began to pray inwardly and to himself.

Whilst lost in thought and deep in prayer, Richard didn't notice the approach of a woman whose footsteps were quelled by the recently mowed grass. When she reached him, she noticed his demeanour of inner-solitude so spoke softly, a tone or so above a whisper. She stood looking down at him.

'Hello Richard…' the young man took his hands from his face and looked up. He recognised Meryl Leigh immediately; she was one of the church wardens, a comely and amiable woman. She continued to speak, 'I hope you're feeling better. When will you be back as our acting priest?'

Richard rose to his feet out of politeness. 'Not for a while, Mrs Leigh,' he answered.

Meryl Leigh was one of Richard's favourite parishioners; the golden-haired Aphrodite of his congregation. She was a good-hearted woman who'd been born and bred in New Milton, so not a snobby, two-faced import from the stock exchange of London. She was the widow of a local farmer and had a beautiful face and soft complexion etched by kindness which belied her age of sixty-three; in fact, Richard was surprised when he found out because she looked twenty years younger. She also maintained the alluring figure of an un-birthed woman half her age.

Meryl spoke again. 'I've been doing the church flowers, taking the old ones away because there's a wedding next Saturday.'

'Anyone I know?' asked Richard.

'Sarah Bagshore and Andrew Collins. I don't expect you know them as they're not regular church-goers.'

'I can't say I've heard of them before.'

'How about you Richard? Isn't it time you found yourself a nice young lady?' asked Meryl.

'I'm quite happy on my own for the time being; maybe when I'm older.'

'Yes, I suppose you are a bit too young at the moment,' said Mrs Leigh.

'And I've got to get better.'

Meryl looked at Richard questioningly with munificent hazel eyes. 'Did you know it was my oldest son who operated on you in hospital?'

The deacon raised an eyebrow. 'I knew the surgeon was Mr Leigh but I didn't make the connection with you.'

Meryl smiled warmly. 'Yes, my son Stephen. He told me it was the strangest operation he'd ever performed.'

Richard looked puzzled; his thoughts dowsed by dubious intrigue. 'Really, why was that?'

Her smile has slipped; she looked serious. 'He told me that somebody else was in the theatre apart from himself and the operating team, someone unseen.'

Now he looked shocked, 'You mean like a ghost?' he asked.

'I don't know. All Stephen was able to tell me was that a powerful force was trying to guide his hands to harm you in some way. So, he had to stop the procedure until he felt it was safe to carry on.' She looked at him earnestly, her words accentuated by sincerity. 'The whole of the operating team felt the evilness of this presence and it frightened them.'

Richard looked thoroughly concerned, his face screwed with anxiety. Could the presence have been one of those butchers he'd witnessed in his dreams? he wondered fretfully.

Mrs Leigh flashed a smile again. 'Anyway, I mustn't hold you up. If you're free later on why not pop into the farm for a cup of tea?'

With that invitation she turned and walked away and Richard, being a man of God, tried to ignore his salacious thinking about the amatory swagger of her curves, so averted his eyes.

But the young deacon was mesmerised by the thought of Meryl Leigh's invitation to enjoy tea with her later that day; he simply couldn't get the idea out of his head because he found her so attractive in so many different ways – charitable and kind added to which was her alluring beauty; truly a Christian cougar and teaser of his chastity! So, he decided to accept the kind offer as he hadn't been out of his flat much recently, other than to the supermarket and Ludlow's surgery, and needed a break from the boredom of repetitive daily procedures.

First, he returned to his flat for an ample dose of whisky evoked courage to repress his reticently shy nature then, fresh-minty-chewing-gum in mouth, left for the rendezvous. As it was such a lovely evening he decided to walk to his destination as the farm was only a mile or so from his place and (as his mother was so fond of saying) the fresh air and exercise would keep him healthy. Meryl Leigh lived in a fine house, almost of mansion proportions; when he arrived, he rang the doorbell and waited. It wasn't long before the door swung inwards and Richard was greeted with a warm, welcoming smile from beautiful Meryl who stood in the door-opening, her hair cocooned within a turban-like towel and her curvaceous womanliness shielded by nothing more than a high-above-the-knee, red-satin gown which hinted alluringly her nudity beneath. He somehow felt compelled to study her form – a conflict of shyness and admiration - awkwardly pulling his gaze from her butter-soft thighs up past the valley of cleavage between her plump breasts to those smiling, non-pejorative hazel eyes. Noticing the blush that was flushing Richard's face, Meryl apologised for her suggestive appearance with a hint of sobriety that clashed with her jaunty features.

'Please excuse what I'm wearing but I've only just got out of the shower,' she said, her kiss-me succulent lips rising welcomingly again, 'Please come inside; I'll get changed into something more suitable and then I'll make us that cup of tea.'

She turned and Richard followed her inside, down a corridor towards some stairs. Before she reached them (the curate tailing in her wake) she opened a door off the passage and passed into a voluminous living-room bedecked by a blue patterned carpet and various chequered rugs. At the far end of the room was a grand-piano (lid open and yawning agape) beside four French doors leading into an orangery, the windows of which were obliterated by bursting tropical blooms and foliage. The rest of the room was beautifully decorated; lower half of the walls panelled in pine, upper halves festooned with ornately-framed paintings and several montage-mosaics of portrait-photos; midst between these was fixed a large flat-screen television above a fireplace with a marble surround like a Greek temple. And hung splendidly from the ceiling were two chandeliers (one at either end of the room) which winked with sunlight that was pouring in from four Georgian-style windows along one flank. Of course, there were the furniture necessities, three leather sofas, two armchairs and a scattering of stripped-pine cabinets smiling with charmingly-wonky drawers; two French-dressers displaying a parade of fine china; vases exploding with blooms stacked on meticulous shelves, coffee tables and a large drinks cabinet with glinting crystal decanters and sunlight shimmering glasses on top. It was a clean, dust and cobweb free environment, one sweetly perfumed by rose-petal potpourri.

'Make yourself comfortable,' said Meryl, motioning at one of the plush sofas. 'I'll go and get dressed,' she hesitated for a moment then looked at him with a flirty twinkle in her eye. 'Or would you prefer me like this?' she asked, wiggling suggestively and indicating that inherent cunningness of a woman's desire.

Richard plunged his behind down onto the soft sofa. Although he was much younger than Meryl, he still found her very appealing and attractive in both her womanliness and personality. So, he knew the answer to her question was in the affirmative but doubted his judgement, his inner sentiment accusing his thoughts with that piously-divine motive common to some churchmen; spicy versus temperance. So, his answer was typically middle-of-the-road and neutral. 'I don't want to put you to any unnecessary trouble.'

Meryl took his reaction as a sober "yes-please-cover-yourself-up" as he still looked a little edgy and ill-at-ease; but she mistook his softly coy nature for one of being a prude which inwardly was a battle he was trying to overcome. But offending him was the last thing she wanted to do as Richard would soon be the parish vicar. 'I'll just put on a dressing-gown then,' she said leaving the room with a seductive swagger and heading for the staircase.

Sat at her dressing table Meryl observed her reflection while applying soft-tints of make-up to her cheeks and eye-lids. She knew she was attractive, daily cavalcades of men's ogles and leers in the street attested to that; and she knew what she wanted from that gorgeous looking young man downstairs. It was difficult to resist the urge as it'd been almost five years since Robert (her husband) had been crushed to death under an overturned tractor and she'd been as celibate as a nun ever since. She had been married to Robert for thirty years, during which time he'd never been the most sexually dynamic man on the planet; always too tired to perform so once a month was average, and then only if she was lucky. She towelled her hair then put on some lacy black lingerie and stockings which she scantily shielded by wrapping herself in a crimson dressing gown, purposely leaving the waist-belt loose so Richard could glimpse the forbidden fruit.

When she walked back into the living-room, with the bottom half of her dressing gown cracked open and her un-brushed tangle of hair looking savagely tantalising like a wind-swept Boadicea, she looked wildly wanton and magnificent to Richard's naive-to-sexual-conspiracy eyes. Then she adjusted the belt around her waist, angling the bait of her desire and demonstrating to him a little ballet of mesmeric female finesse. She looked down at him, 'Would you like tea or something a little stronger,' she asked, that flirtatious twinkle back in her eye.'

'Tea would be fine,' replied Richard a little timidly, still winded by her provocative behaviour.

'Are you sure? The drink cabinet's well stocked.'

The three temptations of Christ, thought Richard; but none of those involved alcohol and Jesus enjoyed a glass of wine. 'I am quite partial to a glass of whisky now and then,' he replied, fibbing uncharacteristically to cover-up his dependence on the drink. It wasn't in Richard's nature to be deceptive, but God had abandoned him as a child and alcohol became his secret coping mechanism to the terrible abuse he'd suffered. Now it was necessitated by those agitated dreams about his pre-incarnate soul, that wretched nuisance of a person (gender unknown) known as Iggy.

Meryl smiled hospitably, disguising guile because she hoped the alcohol would loosen his priggishness and maybe his pants. She crossed the room to the drink cabinet, topped a tumbler with whisky then brought it to him and curled down next to him, her dressing gown carelessly (but on purpose) flailing open beneath the belt, a salacious glimpse of Eden's apple; but she sensed his unease so adjusted the garment, a modest consideration to remove temptation from his eyes. Then she snuggled closer to him and gently laid her hand upon his knee. She had made the first move and Richard got the message loud and clear; confusion versus delight. Should he, or shouldn't he? What would Iggy have done? Those were his initial thoughts before they were dragged down by his father's molesting hands to that place which engendered cautious retreat. Richard Pope had become a martyr to his own virginity, not because he'd wanted to but because of his dreadful past. So, he stood abruptly, bid his hostess a polite parting, then left for home

Meryl Leigh was not seen attending New Milton church again; later that year she sold the farm and moved to Cornwall to be close to her daughter and grandchildren.

CHAPTER 10

On the move again from Ravensbruck to Bergen-Belsen; shooed out by cowardice over the allied advance.

"Milk the cow, never feed her. Milk the cow, never feed her." - Ken Goldstein

Can you imagine being so weightless, ascetic and frail that you could almost levitate and float, that a gust of wind might blow you to the tree-tops like a kite, yet feel so heavy as if you were wearing lead boots and be so exhausted that you just wanted to collapse in a pile of skin and bones, all the time knowing if you did your life would be extinguished by a bullet from an SS gun? Cold and wet, non-stop night and day, trudging forward through puddles and mud like cattle to the abattoir, grubby fingers gnarled into bone-tight claws, shivering within thin rags and sole-less shoes; this was the dreadful circumstances that befell most of the malnourished and overworked prisoners on a death-march and was certainly the case for a German-Jew called Aron Kaufman, a middle-aged man (one of the very few who'd been at Ravensbruck) who'd trudged labouredly day and night within a SS guarded group of over three hundred mostly female prisoners, along the two hundred and seven miles (three hundred and thirty three kilometres) from Ravensbruck to their new posting at the Bergen-Belsen labour camp. And Death himself was there among them, wielding his scythe to topple another victim for the guard's gun, his skeletal visage aglow with a gargoyle-like malicious smirk from within that black cowl; this was fun, he hadn't been so busy since the last World War.

It was night-time, the eyes to the exhausting route-march being the candle-strength glow from the slits within the black-out headlamp masks of a truck behind crawling along to the deadbeat tromp of the prisoners, the timid beams from which flickered black shadows to spin among the group like mockingly-wicked dancing demons. The truck was a troop-carrier so that the guards could swap around and rest in shifts; those currently in the canvas-shrouded back swaddled in blankets, cosily warm and noisily asleep along with three pricked-eared German Shepherds; the dogs were allowed to rest, the Sematic march outside was not. There was also a Mercedes staff-car heading the miserable procession, sat in the rear of which (along with two other SS-Aufseherins) was SS-Rapportfuhrerin Irma Grese, gently asleep with her head resting on the shoulder of her neighbour (Khan was one of the dogs [dozing in rabbit-chase reveries] in the truck following the death-march), her mind swimming joyously with dreams of Franz because they'd be together again as soon as they reached Bergen-Belsen; then another pistol shot slapped the morbid darkness like the crack of a whip; one more prisoner's life extinguished (a female political prisoner who'd once been a distinguished member of the Judiciary of Germany and a mother to four surviving teenagers).

Aron Kaufman slogged on somewhere towards the rear of the lugubrious death-march. At Ravensbruck he'd watched his wife and two children being press-ganged into the gas chamber, so the drudgery of each agonising footstep was a persistent torture of bleakest remorse, a mind-flash of his wife's face, the next step one of his children, the next the other one; an unrelenting sparked suffering until he could take no longer. What was the point of living now? Rumours were that the end of the war was very close but what was there to return to? He had nothing and was stone broke because the SA thugs had burnt his tailoring business and its upstairs living accommodation to the ground during "The Night of Broken Glass" in November 1938. And the zealous Nazi would still hunt the Jew, a relationship like that of the lion and the antelope. No, he hadn't the strength or the willingness to put it all behind him and start again so he dropped down into the squalid mire beneath his slogging feet and a bullet to his head turned out the tormented light of another grief-stricken soul.

Then came that menacing droll hum from the night sky above, louder and louder was the rumble as it neared...then the shout, 'Halt and turn off the lights!'

The procession stopped knowing that enemy aircraft were approaching high above, the heavy and ominous rumble of many bombers, an unseen swarm of propellers shuddering the brooding dark. One or two of the stronger prisoners slipped away into hiding, unnoticed in the absorbing darkness that'd stunned the eyes of the guards to an overwhelming blindness. Irma was jolted awake by the kerfuffle; intrigued she jumped out of the car, her eyes straining in the blackness to follow the drone from above. One moment they were ahead of her, then invisibly rumbling loudly above, then behind her as distant search-lights flicked suddenly on, sending transparent silver tunnels of light streaming up into the night sky; and ack-ack guns started to boom and flash, sparking the heavens like jubilant fireworks. As the rumble faded to a drumming hum, the distant horizon of muddled silhouettes, contrasted against the moon-silvered night, began to bloom with flashes of yellow suffusing into an overall aura of ferocious orange. What was left of Berlin was being bombed again.

In the city itself, a few late-night young revellers were gathered together and enjoying the bouncy, smoke-swirling atmosphere inside a bar; off-duty German soldiers and several civilians, laughing, singing, drunkenly dancing to the piquant notes from a boisterous piano. Beads and bangles, champagne, beer and iron crosses all jingling and cavorting happily to the music; the jolly atmosphere within rang with munificent laughter and cheers, so loud and raucous that they couldn't hear the air-raid sirens or the blasting defence guns. But sixteen thousand feet above them there was a sticky concentration of grave seriousness between the eight-man crew of a British Lancaster bomber (number NX665) that's four Merlin-engine-powered propellers whirled and chopped the booming and flashing blackness before them. The pilot of NX665 gave the order to open the bomb-doors while two others in the twelve-plane squadron dropped flares to illuminate the black-out city below. Moments later, twenty thousand pounds of high-explosive dropped from NX665's belly. The bombs whistled down towards the city; three fell on the bar, the first smashing the piano before exploding. There were no survivors from the thirty-two having fun and enjoying the evening, just a macabre splay of blood-splattered severed limbs and grisly splotches of flesh, just like smashing a melon with a mallet. So, some baby's parents, another's brother, a sister, some child's aunt and uncle, another's cousin...all brutally slaughtered from a dubious innocence.

Back to the death-march: as the threat from above had passed it was safe to proceed towards Bergen-Belsen but still too dark after that forgetful-of-duty delay to undertake a thorough head-count. It was five miles (eight kilometres) further on that the SS officer in charge (travelling in the front staff-car) remembered to do so. These five miles had taken an agonisingly slow two and a half hours to complete due to the weakened, shrunken, chicken-like legs of the prisoners. Now the gloom was beginning to fade to the birth of dawn and he stopped the progress again with a bright red glow from the car's brake lights.

The officer put on his death-head cap and got out of the front of the vehicle. He then proceeded along the four-prisoner-wide wretched shamble of forlorn faces and ragged frames and approached one of the guards at the rear of the pitiful troupe.

The officer spoke to the guard. 'We started with exactly three hundred and fifty,' he said arrogantly as if belittling his subordinate with the status rank. 'How many have fallen by the wayside?'

'Forty-three have been dealt with so far Sir,' replied the guard obediently.

The officer thought for a moment. 'So that means that there should be three hundred and seven left. Help me count them.'

So, the officer and the guard walked between the four lines of the death-march counting each head, a process in the ripening gloom which took almost half an hour. When they'd finished, the officer said to the guard, 'I only counted three hundred and five, how about you?'

'The same amount as you Sir.'

'Fuck it!' growled the officer angrily, 'That means two have escaped.' He paused for thought, 'Two times ten means that twenty must be executed to deter any others from escaping.'

So, the officer randomly selected nineteen of the women prisoners and the only remaining male, pushed them down onto their knees on the grass verge facing away towards a shaggy hedge; he then ordered two machine-gun guards to stand behind them (one at each end if the line) and gun them down. The machine-guns rattled and the blood-splattering line collapsed one by one except for the male in the middle of the line-up, an athletic young man who sprang up from the group and sprinted away in a zig-zag to avoid the flurry of bullets that followed him. This young chap (nineteen years old) was an ostracised and socially excluded gypsy and, unlike the once (pre-war) selfishly-luxuriant and corpulent Jews, had survived a life used to hardship, an anatomy that could hibernate to retain strength in time of famine. He was too fast to chase so the officer ordered another ten women to kneel on the verge for execution, ten more bubbles of life were then popped by the vindictive murderer's weapon. There were no more attempts to escape that death-march although by the time they'd reached Bergen-Belsen, sixty-six more prisoners had collapsed from exhaustion or thirst and were shot in the head where they fell.

*

Now I want to divert from my story, take a short tangent away because what happened to the young gypsy lad who'd escaped the firing squad was lucky and also interesting. His name was Vano Tabor, born in Romania then moved to Germany with his parents when he was a toddler of just two. So, he was influenced by a German education (was fluent in the language with a Bavarian lilt) until Adolf Hitler grasped the country with a savagely puissant and racist ideology when the family, frightened by the madness and tirade-threats of this angry tyrant, moved away and settled in Poland.

Vano's highly-alert, instinctively feral and ear-pricked escape had been made mostly through woodlands, not simply because of the secret cover it afforded him, but also because the morning was a beautiful, bucolic early spring one late in March and the vernal, bursting buds blushing on the thicket of twisted and gnarled branches above and around him played a bouncy orchestra of birdsong; being at one with nature is innately akin to a gypsy psyche, and something Vano's soul had cried out for while enduring the harshness at Ravensbruck; the chatter of magpies, screams from starlings and the coo of the wood pigeon, all while inhaling that jaunty efflorescence of the season. Vano had made excellent progress in a northerly direction towards the coast where he hoped to find passage to the neutrality of Sweden. However, fifteen miles away from his escape from the death-march his plans were about to change. It began as he approached a narrow road, which split the woodland he skulked within into two, where he could hear the approaching mumble of several diesel engines. It was bound to be a German troop convoy so he sunk to the ground lying belly-flat on the peat carpet and waited, peering covertly from behind a bunch of bracken fronds, about fifty yards back from the tarmac strip. As the ashen coloured convoy of six trucks and three motorcycles and sidecars came into view, the stubby, flat-nosed fuselage of an American F6F Hellcat fighter aircraft howled down from the heavens above, swooping over the vehicles like a buzzard after prey, wing-housed Browning machine-guns spitting fire angrily. As the bullets were the canon type that detonate on impact, most of the trucks exploded immediately (fuel tanks ruptured); soldiers spilled out of the two that weren't engulfed by flames like panicked ants from the aardvark (a scene of diving for cover panic) only to be mown down on the aircraft's merciless return, which included four high-velocity rockets which screamed inwards then boomed into the convoy targets with a tsunami of ravaging flame, the heat from which stung Vano's face. It was a massacre from which there could be no survivors as the Hellcat whirled away from the carnage, soaring up and swirling in a victorious loop-the-loop into the morning sky then disappearing over the horizon, the buzzard having mutated into a joyous lark.

Vano couldn't see any movement, no signs of life and he realised that if he could swap his ragged prison garments for a German uniform, the disguise could make his passage to the coast clandestine and easier so long as he avoided any advancing allied forces. So, he waited until the flames subsided to a smoulder before he went to explore because the smoke would shield his movements from any curious enemy eyes that might've been drawn by the sound of the explosions. It was only when he reached the smouldering wreckage of the convoy that he realised it'd been an SS troop movement and that one motorcycle and sidecar (a BMW R75) had survived the Hellcat's onslaught. Those soldiers who hadn't escaped the trucks were horribly burnt - roasted in their metal tomb, but there were at least fifty uncharred bodies scattered around the scene, maybe more so he had a choice of the least damaged uniform. Some were horribly mangled in gore, others weren't so bad and he found one belonging to a corporal which seemed intact and undamaged and, as luck would have it, about his size. Vano hauled the corporal's corpse into the cover of some nearby trees, just-in-case and to avoid being spotted, stripped the body of its uniform, shirt, tie and swastika arm-band, then changed into the military ensemble, the finishing touches being commando-style boots and the corporal's helmet, all of which fitted perfectly. In addition, there was money in the trouser pockets and the corporal's ID papers within the inside jacket pocket, the worn portrait photo on which could easily pass as his own. Disguise complete he approached the motorcycle and sidecar via a bloodied slalom of bullet-torn corpses. As he did so the noticed the bullet-beaten body of an SS officer slumped ingloriously on the ground. He approached the carcass and noticed that the man had ash-blonde hair. This sparked an idea; Vano had a sister called Elena who'd remained at Ravensbruck and who might still be alive as she was employed as an essential worker in the Siemens electrical engineering factory adjacent to the camp. When Vano had been there he'd worked in the crematorium along with another man called Szymon (he didn't know his surname as it was unnecessary) who was Jewish but who happened to have blonde hair (unusual but not unheard of in the Sematic race). The two had become friends before the SS promoted the Jew to a kapo because of his Aryan appearance (which educed a certain sympathetic comradery among the Nazi ranks) and also his methodical efforts to duty. A kapo was a leader among the prisoners (prisoner functionary) and Szymon was posted to the Siemens factory to keep an observant eye on the camp-workers labouring within. Now the corpse on the ground beneath Vano's feet had the three-pip rank of Captain which just happened to be that of the SS commander of Ravensbruck which added a safety surety of equal rank respect. His idea was to take this uniform (a grey one which buttoned up to the neck so no need for a shirt), hide it in the sidecar and take it to Ravensbruck and ask Szymon to wear it in the hope the two of them could get his sister away from the death-camp. Although the uniform was badly damaged from the air-raid, it could be repaired and gypsies, due to the needs of poverty, were artisans in such things. So, he stripped the body of the uniform, belt and holstered pistol, boots and cap (which had been flung about six feet away) took money and the ID wallet from the pockets and stuffed the entire outfit into the nose-cone of the sidecar. But he'd also found, tucked securely into the officer's wallet, a black and white photo (faded to sepia by the insurgence of war) of a woman and two young girls, all smiling contentedly with love, who he assumed were his wife and daughters; this he respectfully slipped into the man's vest, facing inwards next to his heart. To cover his resourceful, but cunning, act from curious eyes, he hauled the Captain's body away from the smoking carnage to a thicket of briars, snapped the dog-tag from his neck and put it in his pocket. He then hid the officer's carcass in the thorns, feeling a sprinkle of sorrow because – whether German, Jew or Gypsy - death is always a relentless grief for those left behind (the faces on the photo); however, the cruelty once meted out to him by the SS quickly evaporated this momentary reflexion, engulfed by an avalanche of revengeful joy. The corpse was now unidentifiable to the questioning eyes which would eventually find it; he did the same with the corporal's body (except he hung the dog-tag around his own neck to add authenticity to the disguise), pushing his corpse into the thorns alongside that of the captain. He hadn't time to rummage through the other corpses for money and valuables for fear of being caught, and so his next duty would be to find somewhere to scrub the blood stains from both uniforms; his one had only a little around the collar but that of the officer's was quite extensive in the stomach area. This washing process was something he hoped to do quite soon as it would be easier before the blood had a chance to fully congeal. So, during his motorcycle ride he would keep an eagle eye out for a pond, brook or river.

Vano had never ridden a motorcycle before and so it was a spluttering stop, stall and start again introduction to the art, one he practised to a novice's mastery before gingerly embarking astride the machine en-route back to Ravensbruck which he estimated was about two-hundred miles (three-hundred and twenty-two kilometres or a four-to-five-hour trip) back from whence he'd come. There was an urgency to save his sister but inevitable delays to wash and repair the German uniforms and also to rest from the night-and-day exhaustion of the death-march. It was late during that beautiful morning when he crossed a narrow bridge which spanned the silver waters of a shimmering brook. As he didn't want to draw attention to himself, he took the motorcycle and sidecar off-road and hid it in a bunch of trees. He then took the officer's uniform out of the nose-cone of the sidecar and followed the stream into a conifer glade where he couldn't be seen from the road. First he squatted down by the brook, cupped his hands and scooped-up some of the sweet water to satisfy his ravenous thirst; then he took off his corporal's jacket and helmet and scrubbed the blood stain from the collar using a pine cone; next he immersed the captain's uniform which blushed the stream's serene transparency in ruby red as he scrubbed; as he did so, Vano studied the jacket, especially the area of damage which was restricted to one side of the lower waist and had not spread elsewhere, so more likely shrapnel from an exploding truck than a bullet from the plane which would've either exploded on impact or travelled right through the garment. Once he'd finished, he spread the officer's uniform out on the bank to dry. It was now time to rest, so he lay back in the grass on the bank and, for the first time since his escape, he put out-of-mind the empty hunger which burned his stomach to reflect upon the impossible and tranquil perfection of his liberty, to breathe-in and imbibe the freedom that had eluded him for such a long time. Kissed by the soothing heat from the sun he fell asleep.

A couple of hours later Vano's eyes crept open, dilating to wide-eyed surprise. No breath-sweating, stench-poisoned walls, no plank-stiff bunk; no SS guards prodding him with a rifle barrel? At first, he thought he was still dreaming; a mind-trick to tease his reasoning as he looked up at the panoply of lime green stippled with black pine-needles dancing in a gentle breeze over him. Then his liberty realisation laughingly awoke; he was free as he hoped his sister would soon be. The officer's uniform was still very damp but he had to press on as the impatient Nazis in the camp were generous with bullets and any delay might endanger Elena's welfare. So, he put on the corporal's jacket, belt and helmet, picked up the officer's uniform and returned to the motorcycle. This time he put the captain's garments into the open cockpit of the sidecar (not hidden in the nose) in the hope that the wind-rush from the speeding machine would form a gushing vortex to help tumble-dry the material. Now there were two priorities to his revised agenda, first was food and second was to find a haberdashery so he could acquire implements to repair the captain's uniform.

"All my life I've always come back to one thing,

My need to feel free and the need to feel the breeze,

The ride provides a freedom this gypsy needs,

Where every road is another blessed memory,

A new experience to carry inside my journey,

A sense of belonging to a familiar tribe,

A brotherhood that goes beyond a bloodline." — Jess "Chief" Brynjulson

CHAPTER 11

Back in 1945, before the growth of supermarkets and high street brands, haberdasheries, hardware stores and tailoring shops were common place in towns and most villages, so it was not long before Vano came across one. He pulled the motorcycle and sidecar up outside and went in where he was nervously greeted by a bespectacled elderly gentleman wearing brown tweeds. It seemed that even the unprovoked German civilians were wary of the Schutzstaffel's harsh reputation. However, Vano was extremely polite which put the shop-keeper at ease. First, he asked for something to eat, explaining that he'd run out of rations and hadn't eaten since yesterday (in fact he hadn't had anything for almost a week). The shop-keeper kindly donated his own lunch being a cold slice of Bavarian beef pie wrapped in silver foil by his dutiful wife. This Vano greedily devoured, hardly stopping to take a breath. When he'd finished, he'd asked the shop-keeper for a sewing kit, some scissors and grey cotton. There was some jacket lining material which he bought (with the money he'd found in the dead corporal's pocket) but nothing in the shop to match that of the exterior cloth of the captain's uniform; but that didn't matter as the captain wore knee-length boots and trousers that extended to the ankle so no one would notice if he cut off the lower trouser leg to scarf a repair on the jacket since the section of trouser removed would be hidden by the leather shaft of the boot.

Shortly after leaving the haberdashery, Vano found an empty barn inside which he could repair the captain's uniform which was now completely dry. Once again, he hid the motorcycle and sidecar, this time behind the building and away from curious eyes. Luckily it was only the lower front right-hand side of the jacket that was damaged and so he didn't have to form eyelets for the buttons, silver ones he carefully removed from the lethal-laceration torn section of the garment. The officer's jacket had four pockets, two breast ones and two waists. Fortunately, that waist one (pocket) on the damaged section could be reused by unpicking the stitches and attaching it to the newly scarfed cloth once repaired. So, he began by cutting away the damaged section of cloth in a neat rectangle, down the flank join-seam (unpicking stitches as he did so,) along the bottom and up the edge by the button-stance to a new seam which he cut back horizontally to where he'd begun and which would be concealed beneath the leather belt. It took him a couple of hours to make the repair from material he'd salvaged from the lower trouser legs and when complete it was almost perfect as if undertaken by a craftsman tailor with a sewing machine.

It was turning into the best day of the year so far, the type that gladdens the heart as Vano mounted the motorcycle again. He kick-started the engine into an ear-pleasing burble and recommenced the journey back to Ravensbruck. Now that he had the hang of the motorcycle and its complicated controls, he really enjoyed the ride towards his destination, through several secret villages and small towns, curled up like hedgehogs from the fox because of the lurking threat of the allied advance. The warm and whistling air was imbibed with a vernal sweetness, the fuzz of awakening foliage and greening verges warmed by the sun giving an aroma like freshly cut grass. It was a wonderfully invigorating smell, one that put a smile on his face and so different from the stench of burnt flesh and faeces he was accustomed to after years of incarceration in death-camps; and all around him birds darted in frenzied flight, eagerly excited by the onset of the season.

There were several barrier-bridged check-points en-route heading south-east, but only the first two were attended and he was casually waved through them both without having to stop. There was certainly now an air of complacency and save-our-own-skins defeat about Germany and he saw very few troops; those he did come across were hurrying south in flustered convoys, most likely for the defence of Berlin.

Before Vano reached Ravensbruck (which he did just after four pm) he read the pocketed ID papers thoroughly and memorised the identity of the dead corporal from whose corpse he'd taken the uniform, this to prepare himself for an inevitable flurry of questions from assiduous guards (as it would turn out, none of this memory precision would prove necessary as German rigour was acquiescent to inevitable and impending defeat). When he reached the gates of the camp he was hastily admitted and not questioned as identity regulations were being ignored and the entire camp was a scene of chaotic bedlam, the SS covering its' tracks before the imminent liberation by the Red Army who they knew were on the doorstep. The camp was almost ablaze; perfectly good tables, desks and chairs being fed to the flames as was the inmate's looted belongings (clothing and shoes, handbags and suit cases) and reams and piles of paperwork. But there was something starkly different about the complex and it took a moment or two for the penny to drop into Vano's intellect; it was the moribund atmosphere, now inert and clean of the bone-meal smoke; the furnaces that had burnt day and night were extinguished, the death-reeking, corpse-consuming crematoria ceased.

Vano rode the motorcycle straight to the Siemens factory where he knew his sister was employed along with his friend, the kapo Szymon. Inside there, a work-place that clanged and clattered with activity, the few SS guards that were on duty rigorously maintained a harsh discipline, their trigger fingers twitchy with nerves at the Russian threat. But Vano's disguise was inconspicuous to their treacherous eyes (just another guard) and he soon spotted his sister working over a munitions machine; despite looking dishevelled, gaunt and dejected, her ravishing beauty, enhanced by gypsy-green eyes and raven-black shoulder-length hair, was like a diamond in a scattering of pebbles. Snow White he'd called her when together in childhood, as apt then as it was now; and she wore an overbearing loveliness that had saved her from the gas chambers many times, a hypnotic charm about her which, to her cruel suppressors, formed an analogy of the fawn or piglet choice for the conscience-stricken and wavering slaughterer – nine times out of ten the swine was killed because the doe-eyed fawn looked so sweet. Vano crossed the factory floor towards her, invisible in disguise and raising no suspicion, not even from his friend Szymon who stood to one side of the room patting his kapo's truncheon into the palm of his hand. Elena ignored his approach for all she saw was the advance of an SS guard, something she was warily accustomed to; but when he stood beside her and spoke softly in a voice she recognised, she managed a limp pleased-to-see-him smile although her eyes remained crisp, stagnant and dispassionate from dubious doubt and the hardship of long-suffering. But when he whispered the reason for his visit, her lips lifted further and her eyes moistened; to get away from here, to escape from Ravensbruck was the answer to her prayers for, like her brother, Elena was riddled with that jaunty gypsy spirit and therefore an ambition for the thrills and extravaganza of life. He then explained to her his plan using an under-his-breath whisper. Once he'd finished, he left to speak to Szymon.

Szymon was resentful of the authority offered by any member of the death's head brigade as he'd seen them mete out so much cruel punishment (and also been on the receiving end himself); but once he recognised Vano he was pleased to see his friend but prudently did not show it for fear of blowing the gypsy's disguise. Vano then grabbed the

Jew by the arm (a grasp of intolerance to match his disguise) then frogmarched him across the factory floor to the outside of the building where they could talk in secret. No guards had been alerted; no one had suspected an intruder as his rough-handling of the Jew was quite the routine method for prisoners to those within the bullying ranks of the SS; luckily he'd raised no eyebrows.

At this point I'd like to remind the reader that both Vano and Szymon had previously been put to work in the crematorium at Ravensbruck and so were well acquainted with its location and layout.

Outside Vano spoke to Szymon. 'I'm getting both you and my sister Elena out of here today.'

'Really?' questioned the Jew, 'How do you plan that?'

Vano looked around clandestinely before he answered. 'I've got another German uniform for you to wear hidden in the nose-cone of that sidecar,' he said, nodding in the direction of the motorcycle. 'Identity papers are in the jacket pocket and he looks a bit like you.' He paused for thought, 'Where would you like me to put it for you to change into?'

Szymon pondered briefly. 'They're not using the crematoria anymore and they plan to knock them down before the Russians arrive. If you put it in the first oven on the left, I'll find it there.' He hesitated briefly, 'But how are we going to get away?'

'Simply walk out of the gate. Your uniform belonged to a Captain so you can be as arrogant as you like if we're questioned.'

The Jew sniggered at Vano's SS mockery. 'And where do we go if we manage to get away?'

'We'll catch a train in the village and travel north towards the coast where we'll board a boat to Sweden.'

'But we'll need money to catch a train,' suggested Szymon awkwardly.

'I've got plenty of money,' replied Vano

'Where?......'

The young gypsy interrupted him. 'From the same place I got the uniforms, I'll tell you later. Now we must hurry up. I'll put your uniform in the oven you asked me to and you can pick it up in a few minutes, then we can collect Elena and get away from here.'

Vano rode the motorcycle and sidecar over to the crematorium and, after checking he wasn't been watched, entered the building and stowed the captain's uniform inside the location suggested by Szymon. He then tried to make himself look useful so as not to draw unwelcome attention. Szymon approached the building covertly from the rear, sidled along the flank then slipped inside unnoticed except by Vano's alert eyes. Soon the Jew emerged wearing the German uniform and the pair headed for the Siemens factory. Inside, those guards that noticed (what they thought was) an SS captain enter the building, snapped to respectful attention. It was easy to rescue Elena, although Szymon prodded her with a luger he'd found in his belt to add authenticity to their guise. When they reached the camp's gates the guards there simply let them pass straight through, no questions, no papers just respectful salutes to rank; there was a resigned aura of unavoidable defeat about the camp, something that was also written on every gloomy German face while they busied themselves by destroying all evidence of the place's true and heinous purpose, preparing themselves to flee from the imminent arrival of the enemy; murderers wearing rubber-gloves tossing while the weapon into the river.

In the village, before boarding the train, Vano purchased civilian clothing and shoes for all three of them. There were no questioning looks from the shop-keepers as several German soldiers had already had the same idea and were disguising themselves as innocuous civilians ready for an incurious getaway from the allied force's scrutiny of their status, especially those from the SS who needed to remain incognito and escape unnoticed and away from questioning about their wicked crimes. After all this was Germany and her natives, especially those who'd taken up arms to support the Fuhrer, had now to save their skins from the inevitable defeat of vainglorious Nazism.

Vano, his sister and the Jew used a redundant railway siding in which to change their clothes; Elena, of course, was not in German uniform but needed to give the impression of an opulent, plaited fraulein and not a ragged gypsy girl. They kept the false IDs (just in case) and took the night train and arrived at the north coastal town of Binz in the early hours of the following day. From Binz they found passage to Malmo in Sweden from where they travelled by foot, bus and car up country to the coastal town of Goteborg. This wasn't easy as they'd left the false papers in Germany and had no transit visas. So, they used the inconspicuous cover of night added to skulking in what cover was available. It took them three exhausting days but they finally found a willing ship headed for the safe sanctuary of the United Kingdom.

At Auschwitz a Jewess named Mala Zimetbauma met Edward (Edek) Galinski, a Polish political prisoner, and a romance developed. They decided to escape together, in the hope of bringing news about the camp to the free world. On June 24, 1944, they escaped from Auschwitz-Birkenau. Galinski disguised himself as an SS officer and pretended to be escorting a Jewish prisoner to work outside the camp. They were caught two weeks later and executed.

*

Spun with shock, Richard Pope was brutally jolted awake from another nightmare. What were those gnarled, bone-tight and grotesquely straggling heaps of hundreds of bruise-blackened scabby corpses, white-eyed with mouths agape in throes of death? Tony Ludlow or someone had to put an end to these fevered visions! This has to stop!

*

Bergen-Belsen Work Camp - Late March 1945.

This was not an extermination camp such as Auschwitz. Belsen was a starvation and slave-labour camp where inmates either died from lack of nutrition or from being over-worked while in an emaciated and shrunken physical state. In 1945 allied bombing raids had prevented most supplies of food or medication from getting through to the complex, and so the conditions within were appallingly filthy allowing a culture of disease to invade and fester. This resulted in an outbreak of typhus which had a devastating effect on the prison population. Typhus isn't choosy as to whom it infects; Franz Hatzinger (Irma Grese's boyfriend) had been posted to Belsen and had been struck down by the disease. He was in the camp's sanatorium, grasped inside the cragged clutches of that feral, skull-hooded menace of death; he would not survive.

"Epidemic typhus has historically occurred during times of war and deprivation. For example, typhus killed millions of prisoners in Nazi concentration camps during World War II. The deteriorating quality of hygiene in camps such as Auschwitz, Theresienstadt, and Bergen-Belsen created conditions where diseases such as typhus flourished. Situations in the twenty-first century with potential for a typhus epidemic would include refugee camps during a major famine or natural disaster. In the periods between outbreaks, when human to human transmission occurs less often, the flying squirrel serves as a zoonotic reservoir for the Rickettsia prowazekii bacterium." Wikipedia.

There is no frenzy of words, no over-description for the scene which confronted the young Irma Grese's eyes as she was chauffeured in the Mercedes staff-car into the Bergen-Belsen labour camp ahead of the death-march; no stench which could affront one's nostrils such as she then smelt, and no amount of Chanel number five could disguise or dilute it; no way to describe the assault on her tender femininity despite what she'd seen at Auschwitz and Ravensbruck. She witnessed Richard Pope's nightmare - *What were those gnarled, bone-tight and grotesquely straggling heaps of hundreds of bruise-blackened scabby corpses, white-eyed with mouths agape in throes of death?* But, unlike him, she smelt the horrendous ammonia of rotting flesh, festering urine and putrefied faeces. With her tenuous knowledge as a one-time trainee nurse, and that also weaned from Ravensbruck and Auschwitz, she knew the disease consequences of those hideous rotting piles of mangled flesh. She realised that the bodies would have to be buried in several mass graves to prevent the spread of diseases such as cholera and typhus, and those who were inevitably already infected would have to be treated with whatever medication and care that was available. From what she could see so far, the camp was simply a slovenly mess of morbid decomposition with an obvious don't-care-a-less attitude from those in charge. She would have to see the Commandant, a man she'd been told went by the name of Joseph Kramer. So as soon as she got out of the car and had fetched Khan from the truck, she went to find him. She was in the first of six compounds which formed the camp, one framed by several low-level tatty white-painted timber buildings; she headed for that unit with a swastika flag fluttering on the façade as it was most usual practise to fly the Nazi emblem outside the headquarters. Irma held a handkerchief to her nose to dilute some of the stench and even the dog was convulsed by fits of sneezing. She approached a guard at the entrance of the building and asked him, with a tantalising flick of her hair, where she might find the Commandant. This man, mesmerized by Irma's beauty, escorted her to Kramer's office.

Inside the Commandant was sat behind a desk and he smiled welcomingly up at her. Kramer had been at Belsen for just over three months having come from Auschwitz where he'd been second only to Baer (taking the role of Commandant if Baer was away.) Despite this, Irma had never met him before. Kramer stood politely; gentlemanly manners and steadfast chivalry conjured by a female presence. He was a tall, dark haired and bushy eye-browed man with a prominent forehead and black eyes sunk within the shadow of his brow like bore holes; to Irma's selective judging he was not a handsome man.

'Hello, you must be Irma Grese?' he asked a little nonchalantly.

'Yes Sir,' Irma replied abruptly and with deference to rank. 'How do you know who I am?'

'We were expecting you and the rumour of your beauty precedes your arrival. Please sit down,' Kramer said, gesturing at a chair in front of his desk. Grese obeyed, squat down like a duck, and the Commandant also sunk down into his seat. 'How may I help you?'

'Firstly Sir, I'd like to know where I can find Franz Hatzinger as we're old friends who served together at Auschwitz?'

Kramer hesitated with his answer and looked concerned. 'He's in the sanatorium I'm afraid, he's contracted typhus.'

'Can I see him?' Irma asked.

'I'm sorry but that place is off-limits to healthy members of staff as we're trying to contain the epidemic.'

Grese looked sadly disappointed but understood; she was also rigorous with her attitude to obeying military dictates. 'In that case may I form a work-party to help clean the camp up and prevent the epidemic from worsening?'

'What had you in mind?'

'I've noticed the heaps of bodies in the compound next door to this one and the smell is atrocious. Can I suggest we get some stronger prisoners to dig mass graves and bury the bodies?'

'If you can find any,' said Kramer, tittering maliciously. 'I'm afraid most of our prisoners are in bad shape because essential supplies such as food and medication aren't getting through to us.'

'I'll only need ten or twelve, I'm sure I'll find enough scattered around the camp.'

'I don't think you'll find them over-eager to help you,' said Kramer chuckling again.

Irma thought for a moment. 'I can bribe them with food as I guess the SS staff members here have plenty to eat.'

'Yes, we do normally, but our supplies here have run dry so we have to send out for food and pay for it ourselves.'

Irma gave the Commandant a gentle smile. 'Well, I'm sure I can afford a loaf of bread every day to feed my work-party if you'll give me permission to put my idea to use.'

'Yes, of course, but only on the condition that you always wear a gas mask when in close proximity to the prisoners.'

'Yes Sir, and thank you for being so thoughtful concerning my welfare.'

Just as Irma was about to leave the room, her hand twisting the door knob, Kramer called across to her. 'Just one more thing before you go;' she swung her attention back at him, an animated sparkle alight in her beautiful and curious blue eyes. 'I probably shouldn't be telling you this but the British and Canadians are only days away from finding us.' He sighed deeply and looked sad, 'You really ought to take the opportunity to get away from here before they arrive. Many of my staff have already gone with my sanction as there's a very real danger posed by the British when they discover the squalor of death here.'

'Why haven't you gone?' asked Irma, her grip released on the door handle.

'I can't as I feel duty-bound to stay and face the consequences. Besides that'd be like the captain deserting a sinking ship and I'm not that sort of man.'

'I can't either Sir; as now I've found Franz, I won't leave him.'

"She was one of the most beautiful women I have ever seen. Her body was perfect in every line, her face clear and angelic, and her blue eyes the gayest, the most innocent eyes one can imagine. And yet Irma Grese was the most depraved, cruel, imaginative pervert I ever came across." - Dr. Gisella Perl

CHAPTER 12

Richard Pope's forearm was finally out of the plaster-cast. He had insured his written-off motorcycle on a "fully comprehensive" basis. Lucky that he had as the insurance company had now reimbursed the financial element of his loss in full, minus a voluntary excess of five hundred pounds (which in reality was compulsory not voluntary.) Now Richard was supposed to have informed the Government's vehicle and driver's licencing agency of his brain injury and its' black-out side effects; but he'd ignored the official advice given him in hospital, opted for a laid-back approach and waited for the relevant authorities to catch up with him. They hadn't yet and the young curate thought, by the grace of God, he might've got away with it. So now he was in the Triumph motorcycle showroom greedily eying up the latest version of his old bike which was spinning slowly around on a rotating circular stand.

It was a beautiful machine, petrol-tank and bikini-like scanty fairings painted in glistening wasp yellow; a bulky black engine-block that oozed power like ripped muscles; the conical and sculptured twists of the exhaust system like the piping from some elaborate wind instrument; the twin bug-eyed headlamps that seemed to wink suggestively at him; the wide rear tyre, like that fitted to grand prix car, etched with an aggressively patterned deep tread which was just super-sexy to Richard's eyes as he recalled the black-leather-suited, sylph-like, busty brunette who'd sat astride the machine, modelling their mutual beauty on the cover of one of his motorcycle magazines. This was a modern-day and sophisticated dream-machine, far removed from the clattering, rickety and struggling old rickshaw-like one Vano had used during his escape from the death-march. For one thing the Triumph had six times the power output of the wartime BMW, such is the evolution of motorcycle engineering over the decades. And this was the bike for him and so he paid the salesman a healthy deposit and asked the man to hold the bike for a few weeks until he was ready to take ownership. Of course, the salesman happily agreed and took Richard's mobile phone number for future use. Now the young curate wasn't irresponsible; he hadn't experienced a brain-seizure incident for a while but was still enduring those terrible nightmares; while they were still haunting his thoughts, he was probably at risk; so, he'd wait for these to cease, wait for the cure to the agitated reveries, before taking possession of his new machine. But somehow this was just a measure of his growing confidence in his recovery, and innately he felt he was nearing the end of the current turmoil.

Richard was due to see Tony Ludlow later that day but was becoming quite cynical about the psychiatrist's help and his bumbling inability to end the nightmares. Without knowing it, his subconscious had screamed for help after the motorcycle accident, a plea to end the anguish over his abused childhood. Irma Grese (his pre-incarnation) had stomped into his nightmares to give him a vision of the malevolent and wretched conditions of extreme squalor and rifle-butt abuse other children had once suffered, those poor mites confined within the swirls of barbed-wire inside a death-camp; those dreadful and turbulent times during the second world war and, like Marley's ghost to Scrooge, bring a scale and unarguable reason to ease his captivated trauma, to calm polluted waters into a clear-water lagoon; to give him a life absent of the shadow of brooding inadequacy resulting from his bullying and abusive father.

But you can only scream for so long before running out of breath; consequently, his attitude towards the awkwardly clumsy psychiatrist had changed; the lips of his cry-for-help were now firmly shut like a clam, the plead-scream sealed like the pout on a marble bust. Furthermore, and as Richard somewhat naively understood the situation, a holy man believed in reincarnation, but pre-incarnation was probably a complete nonsense, a concocted idea by some limelight-seeking professor from America!

As for the issue of the abuse he'd suffered as a small child, this would never stop punishing his intellect for these were scars of the psyche and, like those on the skin, are concrete-set to remind the afflicted of an incident or injury. But unlike scars on the skin, those of the psyche can open up at the slightest provocation, such as a relating news report or some words in a book; then the victim is sent spiralling once more into that dreadful abyss of painful memories he or she has tried so hard to evade. Physical pain from a battle-wound will eventually abate although the dreadful memory of the maiming probably won't. Mental pain from heinous sexual abuse never subsides; it is a dreadful and malignant burden which the victim carries through a troubled life to the grave. But maybe, just maybe, the nightmares about the holocaust (the syringe Mengele stabbed into the fat boy's eyes) gave some perspective to Richard's suffering so that, one day, he would be able to categorise his thoughts into more positive thinking and negate the thirst for alcohol fuelled solace.

Despite the putridly horrendous conditions at Bergen-Belsen, Irma Grese was happy to have been posted there. This was because she could see the comatosed Franz Hatzinger (albeit from within the goggles of her breath-restricting gasmask) through the window from outside the sanatorium block, and watch the bed-sheets rise and fall to his fragile breathing; it was at least some comfort for her lonely and abandoned heart. How she longed to be held in his powerful arms again and to feel him deep inside her. Soon they would be together and wouldn't have to snatch a cosy moment of military-confined privacy anymore; no because soon they would be cocooned together by warm blankets, writhing in intimacy and making-love until the early hours – how her core yearned for the warmth of his touch.

Irma had also organised a work-party of seven women and three men to dig the mass graves required to bury the piles of rotting corpses. This gang had been comprised from the only able-bodied inmates she could find among the thousands still incarcerated at the camp; she had bribed their labour with a share from a fresh loaf of bread she brought every day. But how was she to know that one of the women in the work-party had witnessed her own sister being whipped to the ground by Irma Grese back at Auschwitz? (for arguments sake let's call the woman Mandy for easy reference later on). And how was she to know that Mandy's sister had succumbed to sepsis and died as a result? Revenge for this atrocity (the murder of her sister) was foremost in this Mandy's mind. But Irma hadn't committed homicide on this occasion or even contemplated it. Perhaps (and it's a shallow maybe) she was acquiescent to the charge of manslaughter. But the true reason for the woman's death was due to lack of medical attention, not only by SS medics but also that absent from lackadaisical, frightened-of-infection fellow inmates. However, Irma was ignorant of the consequences she would face over this incident; from her point of view, unlike Mengele and many others, she had nothing to run away from other than her loyalty to the Reich and her unwavering obedience to ruthless orders given by her senior officers.

Irma reluctantly dragged her torpid attention away from the sanatorium-block window, away from the subject of her desire; she shut down dreamy yearnings of her future with Franz and conjured that SS sense of duty and determination which would be so necessary to face the macabre task she and her work-party faced. This was not a woman's work, especially not one with the innate, albeit war-tarnished, but still intricate feminine delicacies of the young Irma Grese. But most of the male German staff stationed at Belsen were either too lazy or too drunk to care, a complacence and inertia mirrored by their commander. Chivalry had deserted most of them and they'd surrendered to the apathy of defeat. Put simply they just didn't care anymore, wanted to return home and be liberated from the years of the Fuhrer's tyranny. Irma too sensed the air of freedom. She sensed the nearing presence of the allied forces, like a forbearing autonomy, wafting closer and closer; however, she felt no serious threat in consequence to her wartime activities.

As she walked a short distance away from Franz, Khan leashed at her side, she was beckoned to turn back by the Commandant who stood at the far corner of the sanatorium. He shouted across the empty, but putridly cloying air between them, from about fifty yards away. 'Fraulein Grese you still have time to get away, save your skin while you can.'

A few weeks, even a few days ago it would've been unthinkable to turn her back on a senior SS officer. But Irma trusted her intuition; she felt safely rebellious and knew her duty was now offered in obedient affection to the welfare of Franz Hatzinger, to clean up Belsen and rid the camp of disease so he could recover. So, she made no reply to Kramer and turned curtly away from him, back in pursuit of gathering the work-party together.

Irma was at a transgression of her womanhood; when she'd entered the SS at the tender age of seventeen, she was still a youth agitated by bitter and alien-to-nature hormones stirred by the child-to-teenager's rebellion at the puberty onset of adulthood added to that acrimonious resentment of her upbringing; her mother's untimely death and her father's cruelty and cold lack of parental guidance. Although an avid Nazi, her father hated the SS and she hated him, so the regiment became her catalyst to join in a feisty "up yours" gesture of defiance. Since the age of thirteen she'd felt like a solitary and tiller-less vessel adrift on a storm-tossed sea. Consequently, it had been down to her to find an anchorage; the tough, military regime within the ranks of the SS had formed that grounding and guidance and also a welcoming comradeship. Now, at the age of twenty-one, she was a beautiful, full-breasted and ripened woman, confident in herself and ready to slip into a second skin, away from the exclusive dictates of men, to emerge as a compassionate female like the struggling metamorphosis of the grub into the butterfly. Her whole life lay before her and, through rose coloured glasses, she dreamed of being with Franz and raising a family within that chocolate-box cottage behind a white picket-fence. Those riding-crop lashes she dealt to inmates at Auschwitz, they had resulted from the pent-up anger stewed-up from her upbringing, a turbulent frustration she'd needed to exorcise by letting off steam with her whip towards which she felt no regret; her victims had always been Jews and it'd been drummed into her that these lesser-beings were enemies of the Reich and deserved the bleakest existence and complete disrespect. All she'd ever known - from a small toddler when those first moments of language had begun to piece-together into a naïve understanding of her gathering world, and on through those impressionable young years when reasoning awakens – were that Jews and Communists were white-eyed monsters that lurked in dark shadows and under children's beds ready to gobble them up. "Fi-Fi-Fo-Fum!" thundered the Jew from the dark abyss of her trusting, yet terrified innocence. Jews and Communists were besmirched and insulted by her mentors at school, on the radio and in the newspapers, a sub-race of vermin which kin and common condemned when speaking to each other using clandestine, hushed whispers. As a child she'd gone with the flow, had no reason to question right from wrong or those brain-wash doctrines of adult Nazi ideology. And through what she'd learnt during the years of war, from the glory of the blitzkrieg through to the verge of defeat, Germany was now standing on the doorstep of ruin and knocking contritely with peace-pacts and bargaining-tools. But racial-hatred had turned-face; most of the world now hated Germany and she was suddenly confronted with the actual "Fi-fi-fo-fum" of the bitter reality of revenge reparations and of an unsure, walking-on-thin-ice and fragilely-insecure future. It was not until now that she began to paddle against the tide because her hibernating personality of womanhood (from youth to adult) had started to hatch and, when surfaced for a gulp of reality above the doctrines of her past and of SS austerity, revealed the feel-sorry-for-them altruistic nature that had saved Alice Tenenbaum (and perhaps many other children) from the gas-chambers.

Irma gathered the work-party together and they began to dig a large pit in the first prisoner compound, adjacent to that occupied by SS staff, using arrow-headed spades she'd found in the stores. Kahn was tied to a nearby post and sprang at the workers back and forth like a tethered yo-yo, barking with bared teeth, his animated tail curled upwards excitedly. Irma helped to dig and worked as hard as those in her charge. This time she was applied and compliant to duty, urging on those she worked with through kind encouragement and with plenty of breaks from work when she, and a couple of other women from the group, brought hot surgery coffee (for energy) from the SS kitchens and distributed them among the group. From Irma's point of view this was a practical boost to elicit the group's generous labour, not an attempt to garnish her personality with kindness or to curry favour for character-reference in light of the allied advance.

It took the team of eleven (including Irma) four days to dig a four-foot-deep pit which was approximately forty feet long by eight feet wide. The group was exhausted by the time it was completed; they would not be able to dig any more until blisters had healed and some strength had slithered back into the remnants of their muscles. But they felt invigorated by the achievement and exercise, thankful for the bread and coffee and all were willing to have another go once they felt able.

But first the corpses had to be interned within the one they'd just finished, not arduous work as the emancipated bodies were just shrunken skin clung to bone with no muscle-mass for rigor mortis to seize and stiffen. So, one by one along a chain they passed each of the skeletal remains, dragging one after the other from the first of the many piles of corpses down into the pit, where each bruise-blistered carcass slumped and straggled against one-another like piles of gnarled twigs ready for the bonfire. And that's what they decided to do; after all, if any relative had survived those poor wretches knotted together in that sump forming a grotesque web of bone-tight, bruise-blackened flesh within the hollows of the pit, they couldn't be identified; nor could those from the many heaps of bodies piled up around the camp. Much simpler to use the pit as a mass incinerator and keep the flames stoked with the tinder of dry human remains; the congealed blood that once coursed the veins, the bones dry as brittle sticks and the skin pulled tight like parchment; bone-tight human pelts parched like chamois and left to dry through lashing winds and winter frosts like smoked kippers in a fish-flake. Just a few splashes of petrol or diesel syphoned from cars or trucks was needed and those wraiths of previous affluence, their once pie-faced wives and pre-war plump children, were set alight in the festering cauldron along with virulent bacteria, germs and any other disease inducing microbes ready to infect and spring-upon the hitherto unpolluted; those lucky ones still clinging to life and who huddled together in refuged shivering communes inside the prison blocks.

114

A couple of days later the British and Canadians entered Bergen-Belsen to liberate the camp. The Officer in charge was Major Leonard Berney of the British Armoured Division along with a selected scattering from other regiments. The Major had been tipped off to the camp's exact whereabouts by a reconnaissance squad of just two men from the Special Air Service (SAS), Lieutenant John Randall and his driver. To think you've been to the fiery depths of hell and witnessed the worst horrors of warfare, and then suddenly find it rudely surpassed, asleep and un-expecting; to dream of the fiend then find yourself met by his snake-like eyes; sitting on the edge of a flaming precipice then getting pushed into a wide-eyed reality that stuns the calculation of reason due to a hammer-blow of shock. Not one of the liberators was immune to this ravishing of their outraged reasoning when witnessing the conditions at Bergen-Belsen. And along with the army were several inquisitive and in-the-way, nuisance journalists armed with flashing cameras not guns. One of the more esteemed among these was the BBC war correspondent, Richard Dimbleby. Shell-shocked by the explosion of depravity and of one race's cruelty and ethnic hatred to another (German to Jew) he made the following radio broadcast and account on entering the camp:

"I picked my way over corpse after corpse in the gloom, until I heard one voice raised above the gentle undulating moaning. I found a girl, she was a living skeleton, impossible to gauge her age for she had practically no hair left, and her face was only a yellow parchment sheet with two holes in it for eyes. She was stretching out her stick of an arm and gasping something, it was 'English, English, medicine, medicine,' and she was trying to cry but she hadn't enough strength. And beyond her down the passage and in the hut, there were the convulsive movements of dying people too weak to raise themselves from the floor.

Cesspit 2a. In the shade of some trees lay a great collection of bodies. I walked about them trying to count; there were perhaps 150 of them flung down on each other, all naked, all so thin that their yellow skin glistened like stretched rubber on their bones. Some of the poor starved creatures whose bodies were there looked so utterly unreal and inhuman that I could have imagined that they had never lived at all. They were like polished skeletons, the skeletons that medical students like to play practical jokes with.

At one end of the pile a cluster of men and women were gathered round a fire; they were using rags and old shoes taken from the bodies to keep it alight, and they were heating soup over it. And close by was the enclosure where 500 children between the ages of five and twelve had been kept. They were not so hungry as the rest, for the women had sacrificed themselves to keep them alive. Babies were born at Belsen, some of them shrunken, wizened little things that could not live, because their mothers could not feed them.

One woman, distraught to the point of madness, flung herself at a British soldier who was on guard at the camp on the night that it was reached by the 11th Armoured Division; she begged him to give her some milk for the tiny baby she held in her arms. She laid the mite on the ground and threw herself at the sentry's feet and kissed his boots. And when, in his distress, he asked her to get up, she put the baby in his arms and ran off crying that she would find milk for it because there was no milk in her breast. And when the soldier opened the bundle of rags to look at the child, he found that it had been dead for days.

Cesspit 4a. There was no privacy of any kind. Women stood naked at the side of the track, washing in cupful's of water taken from British Army trucks. Others squatted while they searched themselves for lice, and examined each other's hair. Sufferers from dysentery leaned against the huts, straining helplessly, and all around and about them was this awful drifting tide of exhausted people, neither caring nor watching. Just a few held out their withered hands to us as we passed by, and blessed the doctor, whom they knew had become the camp commander in place of the brutal Kramer.

I have never seen British soldiers so moved to cold fury as the men who opened the Belsen camp this week, and those of the police and the RAMC (Royal Army Medical Corps) who are now on duty there, trying to save the prisoners who are not too far gone in starvation."

Brigadier Llewelyn Glyn-Hughes, a medical officer, was in command of the relief operation. He said as follows:

"The conditions in the camp were really indescribable; no description nor photograph could really bring home the horrors that were there outside the huts, and the frightful scenes inside were much worse. There were various sizes of piles of corpses lying all over the camp,

some in between the huts. The compounds themselves had bodies lying about in them. The gutters were full and within the huts there were uncountable numbers of bodies, some even in the same bunks as the living. Near the crematorium were signs of filled-in mass graves, and outside to the left of the bottom compound was an open pit half-full of corpses. It had just begun to be filled. Some of the huts had bunks but not many, and they were filled absolutely to overflowing with prisoners in every state of emaciation and disease. There was not room for them to lie down at full length in each hut. In the most crowded there were anything from 600 to 1000 people in accommodation which should only have taken 100.

There were no bunks in a hut in the women's compound which contained the typhus patients. They were lying on the floor and were so weak they could hardly move. There was practically no bedding. In some cases, there was a thin mattress, but some had none. Some had draped themselves in blankets, and some had German hospital type of clothing. That was the general picture."

No sooner had Major Berney, and half a dozen of his men, secured the disarmament and hands-up-in-surrender of Commandant Joseph Kramer, and those ancillary staff within the camp's administration centre (locked them inside the building with armed guards), Mandy sprang upon the British Officer and assaulted him with a bitter complaint about her sister's death at the hands of an SS Aufseherin stationed here at Belsen, a wicked woman who went by the name of Irma Grese. She described Irma's features and probable whereabouts while clinging to Berney in a semi-delirious and grovelling plea for his attention, a teary-eyed annoyance he was forced to heed with that stiff-upper-lip nonchalance of an English gentleman; a wistful audience despite the fact that he, at that particular moment, had much more important matters to attend to. But to appease her hysteria (simply to shut her up), he dispatched a scout of two men to find Grese, place her under house arrest for the time being, then confine her to quarters and lock her inside. When they found her, Khan was shot before her eyes.

Later on, during that first day of liberation, a group of fifteen British nurses (from the Queen Alexandra Imperial Military Nursing Service) wandered into the camp summoned by Major Berney's urgent request for medical expertise. Among them was a young Junior

Sister, a two-pip lieutenant called Brenda King (from my book "On Either Side") who just happened to be deeply in love with a brave SS Major named Karl Wulf, a man awarded the coveted Knights Cross of the Iron Cross and whom she saved from life-threatening wounds inflicted at the Battle of Caen in Normandy. When recovered, Karl was sent to England as a POW where she visited him when on leave. Small world! Even smaller now due to the eighty-five million who'd lost their lives during this conflict.

And later on, among those undignified and anonymous piles of festering corpses within their morbidly etiolated shadows, would lie the body of the diarist Anne Frank, her young frame spent of ambition and promise.

Among the liberators was a young British officer named Dirk Bogarde who would later become a movie icon. This is what he had to say about the camp in a later interview:

"I think it was on the 13th of April—I'm not quite sure what the date was" [it was the 15th] "—in '44 when we opened up Belsen Camp, which was the first concentration camp any of us had seen, we didn't even know what they were, we'd heard vague rumours of what they were. I mean nothing could be worse than that. The gates were opened and then I realised that I was looking at Dante's Inferno, I mean ... I ... I still haven't seen anything as dreadful. And never will. And a girl came up who spoke English, because she recognised one of the badges, and she ... her breasts were like, sort of, empty purses, she had no top on, and a pair of man's pyjamas, you know, the prison pyjamas, and no hair. But I knew she was girl because of her breasts, which were empty. She was I suppose, oh I don't know, twenty-four, twenty-five, and we talked, and she was, you know, so excited and thrilled, and all around us there were mountains of dead people, I mean mountains of them, and they were slushy, and they were slimy, so when you walked through them ... or walked—you tried not to, but it was like .... well you just walked through them, and she ... there was a very nice British MP [Royal Military Police], and he said 'Don't have any more, come away, come away sir, if you don't mind, because they've all got typhoid and you'll get it, you shouldn't be here swanning-around' and she saw in the back of the jeep, the unexpired portion of the daily ration, wrapped in a piece of the Daily Mirror, and she said could she have it, and he [the Military Police] said 'Don't give her food, because they eat it immediately and they die, within ten minutes', but she didn't want the food, she wanted the piece of Daily Mirror—she hadn't

seen newsprint for about eight years or five years, whatever it was she had been in the camp for. ... she was Estonian. ... that's all she wanted. She gave me a big kiss, which was very moving. The corporal [Military Police] was out of his mind and I was just dragged off. I never saw her again, of course she died. I mean, I gather they all did. But, I can't really describe it very well, I don't really want to. I went through some of the huts and there were tiers and tiers of rotting people, but some of them who were alive underneath the rot, and were lifting their heads and trying .... trying to do the victory thing. That was the worst."

"Riches, prestige, everything can be lost. But the happiness in your heart can only be dimmed; it will always be there as long as you live, to make you happy again.

Whenever you're feeling lonely or sad, try going to the loft on a beautiful day and looking outside. Not at the houses and the rooftops, but at the sky. As long as you can look fearlessly at the sky, you'll know that your pure within and will find happiness once more." - Anne Frank.

"For the greatest part of the Jews liberated at Bergen-Belsen, there was no ecstasy, nor joy at liberation. We had lost our families, our homes, we had no place to go, nobody to hug. Nobody was waiting for us anywhere. We had been liberated from death, and the fear of death, but not from the fear of life." - Hadassah Bimko

"I am not trying to write a ghost story but, whilst I tip my hat in tribute to the doubting mists of time, I personally, like many others, have experienced the unexplained which might be interpreted as supernatural; that sighting of a spectre or the thwarted drift of death after calamity. Such happenings evoke the onset of a probing process which pollutes one's thoughts for evermore - the birth of a maverick mind - a riotous rebel to reason which questions the blind acceptance of inculcated evidence, an inquisitive insanity of the known. In other words, it queries the thinking of those who once laid down the foundations of the accepted doctrines and beliefs which form the guidelines of our existence; they could be wrong. For instance, the Theory of Evolution which can't explain the chicken and egg enigma, nor can it clarify where the first spark of life initiated, or indeed, where it drifts to on death. To the un-muddled mind of limited boundaries (a trust of ears and eyes only), a straight-thinker's creed of acceptance ruled by computer-data and scientific theories is conservatively set-in unquestioning stone; to he or she death is a closed door, the finale of one's existence. To the maverick mind Earthly life is just a maggot, death the beautiful metamorphosis into the butterfly; life after life and the acceptance of a realm beyond that which we inhabit." - From my book "On Either Side Part 2."

As mentioned before there is a multitudinous time-warp scale between the pre-incarnate and resurrected worlds of the past and present (here I refer to those incalculable lapses between Irma's and Richard's existence) – some say that a thousand years will pass on Earth to every minute in the otherworld, others ten thousand in that beyond-life eternal sanctuary (hiccupped by reincarnations) most of us aspire that the spirit of our inner-being to ascends up into on death; of course no one really knows as the life after life phenomena (resuscitation from death) is vaguely curtained by the amnesia of one's demise into an unexpected revival of muddled hopes fought over by the pugilists of sadness and pain-free elation; those we're leaving behind and our sparse enjoyments versus a perfect utopia of freedom from poison, worldly grief and bureaucratic irritations; the slashing of Gulliver's frustrating and conformist, governmental red-tape tethers against those moments of delight and the sweet nuances of love we nurture to watch bloom like exotic orchids.

Although Irma had only served for a few days as an SS Aufseherin at Bergen-Belsen before the liberating British turned up, Richard's nightmares about this death-camp had slipped solemnly by and lasted for almost eighteen months. So, while it was still early in 1945 for young Iggy, the year had moved on to late 2014 for her resurrected soul, that now commandeering the psyche of Richard Pope who was approaching his twenty-sixth birthday. Because of his belief in God (and his son, The Saviour Jesus Christ), he had not abandoned the deep-rooted ambition to become a priest, although the thought to embark upon another career had crossed his mind and tempted his reasoning due to that powerful influence (more nagging interference) from the Bishop to keep attending the weekly therapy sessions with the psychiatrist, Tony Ludlow. So, to keep on course he went along with the Bishop's demands, although he found that Ludlow's procrastination and ludicrous theories, siphoned from various dubious and innocuous sources, tiring, and after a while as repetitive as a warped record or badgering hag. Additionally, and the longer he got to know Ludlow, he couldn't help thinking that to treat people with serious mental disorders, a psychiatrist would've experienced some symptoms of contagious mental health themselves so were likely to be as equally doolally as the patient (if not more so)!

Although seasoned to the recurring nightmares, and reluctantly accepting that they could be reflections of his previous life as a Nazi concentration camp guard, Richard still depended on strong alcohol to stun his virulent and vividly animated mind when asleep and help stem those horrific dreams to a trickle, like a beaver's dam to a torrent. But more frequently, when in a spasm of shut-eyed solitary thinking, he imagined he was travelling on a bus and saw a young and proud, blonde woman dressed in a smart military uniform waiting at a stop on the pavement. It was a strange and slightly disturbing recurring vision, the image of a black and white, sepia-yellowed beautiful young woman, surrounded and engulfed by a kaleidoscope of radiant colours. Lured by her exquisite loveliness he waved at her like a demented aircraft controller with flags; but she didn't notice him as the bus trundled past, frustrating his need-to-know-more intrigue to an altogether new and heightened degree. Furthermore, the young man realised he'd have to keep his head down as New Milton's priest in waiting, keep a low profile and always show smiley-faced sobriety to his mentors and those brown-nosed parishioners he encountered at the shops or elsewhere (like Meryl Leigh) whose innocuous and intrusive scrutiny over his welfare secretly irritated the unobtrusive and impartial characteristic of his temperament. So, he was more controlled and clandestine with his consumption of alcohol and would never now dream of riding his motorcycle when even slightly tipsy – he'd learnt that lesson the hard way! He'd also been lucky, had somehow slipped through the Driving Agency's net and avoided the mandatory suspension of his licence normally dependent upon the green light given by medical experts. He simply couldn't take any chances as his love of motorcycling was a mind-calming meditation of escapism for his occasionally wayward temperament, a joyous activity that came a close second to his faith.

Author's note: To prove a detachment from racial bias, I think at this stage I should throw my ethnic hat and a little cultural background into the mix. This is an attempt to prove my distance and impartiality from the rights and wrongs written about in my little, fictional story. Simply put, my stance is neutral and harbours no prejudice.

Though much of this story is unbelievable to modern thinking, most of those horrific incidents within the death-camps are recorded in history, although perhaps a little embellished by latter generations and this writer's overly zealous licence. To counteract, it must also be said that the opposite may be true, that the unmentionable horrors of holocaust were far worse, indescribable and too bewildering to the cultured twenty-first century ignorance and remain with the tacit-lipped victims to the grave. As for the blinkered who postulate holocaust-denial theories, they might as well refute the sun, moon and stars since the evidence of such is unreachable and witnessed by the eyes and ears only, yet closed to the here-and-now of a shallow-thinker's stubbornly-insular reality; horrors of the final-solution are still related by dwindling survivors and, unlike the sun, moon and stars, the evidence is touchable and lies within the ghostly ruins of some death camps left standing in a sad tribute to the millions who suffered and perished and which can be visited by those with a strong stomach (of which I'm not one).

"If you look to the future with one eye on the past you are blind in one eye. If you keep both eyes on the future and none on the past, you are blind in both eyes and may God have mercy on you."

I am and English swing-voter of no political bias as I possess a dissident mind averse to rules; however, I am fiercely patriotic if a little envious of some Americans. Racially my blood swills with neither Jewish nor German heritage (although some sifted Germanic corpuscles may be swimming somewhere within my genes from the Saxon invasion of England way back in 450AD). As far as Vano and the gypsy link is concerned I'm not guilty and, as the Americans say, plead the Fifth Amendment!

Now both Irma and Richard shared a common link, that shameful and keep-to-yourself secret element of child abuse which can colour the afflicted in different ways. Richard, quietly and sombrely, pursued and practised his religion by enveloping his psyche in a shell of forgiveness and those hopeful and insular prayer-meditation beliefs uttered in spiritual privacy to God the Father, God the Son and God the Holy Spirit. It is similar to that optimistic speculation and undoubting gratitude someone experiences when cheating death by a bullet (in this case child abuse) but whose head is grazed by the projectile; the optimist is thankful because had the shot landed an inch further inwards, it would have pierced his or her cranium and they would most likely be dead, ergo that the groping fingers of the fiendish molester may have moved on from the genital area to throttle and silence his victim to prevent a tell-tale witness. The pessimist's thinking is a protest against themselves and their luck, by thinking that if they hadn't been there or if that had the damn bullet had been an inch further outwards it would've missed them altogether! So, no need for people to enquire about his or her wound and fuss like a clucking mother hen over their welfare; a child's fear of the deviant child-abuse monster often buttons their lips, an erosive state-of-mind, almost a foolish embarrassment, that remains conditioned to silence into adulthood. In that initial instant of realisation that they'd just been shot (that act of wrongdoing), none of them question who really fired the gun or why; is history to blame? Was the molester once themselves molested? It is a question that settles and burgeons into a child victim's resentment with maturity, along with the understanding of civilized right from wrong.

Richard's abuse as a child was different from that suffered by Irma. Both were inappropriate and uninvited, but his type was the touchy-feely physical exploitation by an adult of a child's unpolluted innocence. Her abuse by her father was one of mind-control and bullying, one she could try to counteract later on with the solid grounding of a career direction and the emotional strength over adversity offered by military discipline. But they both had suffered the unthinkable as children and each displayed a different coping mechanism, although through the process of reincarnation they both shared the same spirit in a schizophrenic twist of fate, like the one-upmanship of some identical twins where one's the screaming sergeant major, the other a pious monk; Auschwitz concentration camp versus New Milton Parish Church. But in Irma's defence to the inmate-control-methods she chose to adopt in the death-camps (much of which reflected her own violent childhood), she was clenched by that vehement recklessness common to the young and knew no different, followed orders and played an obedient role in the cruel drama she witnessed daily. The right from wrong she'd learnt from a very young age had been indoctrinated by the teachings and propaganda of the Nazi party which contaminated the nationalist majority in the wake of World War One, a dust-yourself-down and get-on-with-it ambitious ethos of German-pride and determination overseen by a madman; the right was returning the fatherland back to the glorious empire snatched away by the Versailles Treaty after the defeat repercussions imposed by the allies following 1914-1918 conflict*; the wrong were those who stood in the way and hindered the progress of the Aryan master race, mainly Semites and Communists.

*The Versailles Treaty forced Germany to give up territory to Belgium, Czechoslovakia and Poland, return Alsace and Lorraine to France and cede all of its overseas colonies in China, Pacific and Africa to the Allied nations.

Kindness is the key to good parenting, to sculpture the clay of a child's personality with gentle hands and loving pride; a little sugar to off-set and sweeten their inevitably bitter

124

voyage-of-life discovery. This acts like a shield to protect against the harshness of reality, is often a relay-baton passed on to the next generation and bolsters self-belief and inner contentment. Without this, at best an individual grows up to be rebellious and untrusting and steps cautiously through life as if it were a mine-field, at worst he or she becomes an unsocial aberrant.

Another author's note: As you might've guessed I was a victim of child-abuse over fifty years ago. I won't go into details but can tell you, with all honesty, that it is a malicious phantom that haunts the intellect and mistrusts the good intentions and kindness of others by assertive qualms, with the exception of those you hold nearest and dearest (in my case my children, to whom I've chosen to divulge little or nothing about the pollution of my upbringing.) And when you let your guard down and believe the ghosts of uninvited memories have been absorbed by the mists of time, they pop back up to kick you, triggered-off by the slightest adverse incident that connects with your personal story, an awful truth to wreck denial. Recently for me (January 2020) it was a court case where I had to sit on a jury and hear both the prosecution and defence of a man, a respected businessman and pillar of society, who was accused of child abuse by a young woman. The incidents (there were eight counts) had occurred over twenty years previously when she was a minor aged under twelve. This case was like reliving my past and I felt the turmoil and frustrated despair the young woman had experienced in the past, and very evidently still did; and I shared every tear this woman spilt as my childhood came rushing back like a bore tide with a following wind. In consequence, once the case was over, I curled up at home, tongue-tied but feeling bleak, somehow guilty and totally wretched because those wounds I'd thought had healed were opened up and agonising again. Unlike Richard I am not dependent on alcohol but could easily become so were it not for my career as a lorry driver. Nonetheless, that earlier section relating to early childhood in a boarding school and hiding whisky in a shampoo bottle is regrettably true. I hope this example gives a hyphened actuality or underlines the trauma of child-abuse.

Irma Grese was pushed from pillar to post by her British captors; they had neither knowledge of her calamitous upbringing nor any appetite to learn about it. All they knew was what they'd seen, and so judged her wrongly upon the few days they'd witnessed she'd spent amongst the appalling squalor of death that impregnated and infested Bergen-Belsen. She was confined to quarters (under guard) every evening at 5pm (1700 hours) and released at 7am (0700 hours) the following morning. Come rain or shine, during the day she was required to help other SS guards, male and female, with the camp clean-up operation, burying hundreds upon thousands of typhus and diphtheria infected decomposing corpses and sanitising the prison blocks where a few surviving inmates clutched tentatively to fragile strings of life. Many of them (around fourteen thousand) were simply too frail and spirit-broken to survive despite their liberator's best efforts; and among them was the seventeen-year-old sister of Anne Frank, Margot who'd survived the brutality of Auschwitz but whose unnourished frailty and betrayed sensibilities of lenient forgiveness succumbed to cruel neglect and to the virulent and putrid diseases at Belsen.

The British paid no respect to Irma's SS rank or status, such as that they grudgingly afforded the German male officers at the camp, and showed no kindness or chivalry towards any of the women other than the most basic guidelines laid down by the inadequate terms of the Geneva Convention; items of personal hygiene, perfumes and make-up were strictly forbidden and food sparsely rationed as a replicate suffering and comeuppance against that imposed by the Nazi regime upon the inmates, both living and dead.

Following a formal interview by a French reporter (one witnessed by a British newsman and which was said to be an angry tirade of accusation by the Frenchman), Irma Grese is alleged to have been shaken to tears by his furious and brow-beating attitude and supposedly answered his barrage of questions with a naively defensive statement of the sort you'd expect from someone so tender in years and reticent of experience. When the Frenchman yelled, "Why did you do these things?" the former SS woman flung her reply to his verbal bullying back emphatically, "It was our duty to exterminate anti-social elements, so that Germany's future would be assured." It seems that this here-say cocktailed with other rumours condemned the beautiful young woman to her fate.

In the middle of June 1945 Irma Grese was formally arrested for war crimes. She was taken from Bergen-Belsen and imprisoned in the town of Celle, a few miles south of Bergen in Lower Saxony.

Without realising it, Richard Pope had somehow connected with Irma's plight. He felt the need to shut himself away in isolation from the pandemic infection of his uninvited but flourishing imagination relating to the pre-incarnation. It was as if he was locked away with her, could feel her remorse for the past and trepidation about the future.

*

It was cold and dark in Irma's tiny goal cell, her only contact with the outside world was that of the infrequent and unwelcome guards who pushed food and drink through the unyielding bars that sometimes enclosed her psyche with an inherent foreboding of trouble to come. But at other times she was more optimistic and blithe-spirited. After all she'd not really done anything too terrible (not like Doctor Mengele), so no more than a slap on the wrist was deserved for her misguided obedience in following the orders of her superiors. But she hadn't had any choice, had she not done so woe-betide the consequences. And she longed to see Franz again; thoughts of him warmed her core from the dank shadows that swam around the little room, changing with the time of day and flickering sunlight like dancing harlequins until swamped by the whelming gloom of nightfall.

And from his self-imposed captivity Richard felt her tingles of hope and shudders from the doldrums of despondency in an ethereal and incarnate telepathy of their spirits. Given the circumstances Irma faced - those of being incarcerated for the first time and pruning the green-shoots of adult life for alleged war crimes she thought should be blamed on others - she understandably fell deep into the empty depths of hopelessness now and again, a state of mind that verged upon depression. And Richard sensed her wretchedness, wanted to reach out to the beautiful young woman who appeared like a lamenting spectre in his solitary musings. When he couldn't oust those images from his mind he reached for the whisky bottle, a trusty friend needed to drown the sorrow plaguing his graphic imagination.

Irma was held at Celle for a few months while the British hurriedly patched together a prosecution case against her (and others accused of war crimes.) They also prepared for the trial by adapting a former gymnasium to a Court House in the nearby town of Luneburg. She was moved from Celle to Luneburg just before the trial proceedings were due to commence on 17th September 1945. (The defendants were 45 former SS men, women and kapos [prisoners with charge over other inmates] from the Bergen-Belsen and Auschwitz concentration camps). Irma and all the others were told, in no uncertain terms, that they would all be facing trial for alleged war crimes. Men and women prisoners were segregated; women gaoled on the first floor and men confined on the second. Irma's cell was among a row of small, temporary cages (more like those suited to zoo animals, overt and missing the dignity of much privacy) interlocked alongside each other and sited on one side of a narrow, dingy corridor through which ran a make-shift row of naked lightbulbs, haphazardly fixed to the ceiling and strung along together by a loose wire, dangling between fixings like the grab ropes along the flank of a lifeboat. At night these gave a spectral and maleficent glow to the faces of the incarcerated, half aglow in an insipid saffron-yellow, the other half sunk in coal-black shadows. But Irma was lucky because her cage was adjacent to that of Elisabeth Volkenrath, her fellow SS enlistee and friend she'd met at Auschwitz and who'd also been evacuated to Belsen. They chatted to each other to keep their minds off the predicament each faced, and played childish games to relieve the boredom of the enclosed, unable-to-exercise restrictions.

One evening quite late, not long after they'd both arrived at Luneburg, Irma's nerves and resolve were a little fragile and raw. So, with her face pinned between the bars of her cage and looking at Elisabeth, who was sat on her table-like (and stiff-as-a-board) bed, she asked, 'Have you any idea what the British will do to us? I mean will we be shot?'

Surprised by the question, Elisabeth whimpered a half-hearted snigger, her profile gilded by the flicker of corridor lights. 'I very much doubt that Iggy. They're very keen on adhering to the Geneva Convention so we'll be treated fairly.'

'Do you think we'll go to prison?'

'Why should we?' Volkenrath replied, a little defensively. 'We've only done what we were told to do. Had we not we might well have been shot by our own side for disobedience or being a traitor to the Reich's cause,' she gave a slight, pepping smile of encouragement, 'No we won't be shot, at worst a few weeks in gaol I expect.'

'But I've already been locked-up and confined for months,' protested Grese. 'Why can't they just fine us and have done with it? After all the war is over and everyone just wants to go home and live-in peace.'

'Well, they've got to save face and be seen to do something.' She hesitated for thought, 'I imagine the surviving Jews are stirring the hornet's nest and causing trouble for us.' Elisabeth looked stony-eyed, her face one of spiteful malice, 'The Fuhrer was right, we should've eliminated the whole bloody lot while we had the chance.' She gulped back her words as an English guard sauntered past in the corridor outside. He glanced in at them, a scowl of condemnation on his war-wizened face.

Had he overheard us? Irma thought; how was she to know he was the product of back-street education so didn't speak a word of German.

CHAPTER 14

"The Blonde Beast of Belsen; The Angel of Death; The Beautiful Beast; The Hyena of Auschwitz:"

The trial of Irma Grese; perhaps more generally, revenge by those with an axe to grind against The Third Reich.

There seems to me to be a basic hypocrisy in the Western legal system, more so back in 1945 than today. Plaintiffs, defendants and jurors are required to give a sworn oath before trial proceedings commence. Many give this oath with their hand grasping a Holy Bible, a gesture denoting their belief in the Christian religion and therefore the various teachings within the book they hold. Of course, it also heightens their status to some of the pious involved in the proceedings, wraps a halo around their unsullied nature and wholesome clean-living; a goody-two-shoes moral righteousness which most agitated cynics are dubious about. That aside, some of the basic teachings of the Bible are about forgiveness of sins, or crimes if you prefer:

Luke 6:37

"Judge not, and you will not be judged; condemn not, and you will not be condemned; forgive, and you will be forgiven."

Matthew 6:14-15.

"For if you forgive men their trespasses, your heavenly Father will also forgive you. But if you do not forgive men their trespasses, neither will your Father forgive your trespasses."

Luke 23:34

On the Cross, Jesus said, "Father, forgive them, for they do not know what they do."

Lastly, of course, the ultimate betrayal of forgiveness is being sentenced to death; number six of the Ten Commandments *"You shall not murder."*

However, you look at it, the death penalty is murder because it is a calculated act of revenge not an accident, something some countries still practise with a callous impunity. It is an unnecessary and sweeping-aside vengeance, a good-riddance-to-bad-rubbish policy, a sentence which is only too often found to be wrong due to the evolutionary wheels of evidence.

And yet, for those found guilty of a crime there seems little leniency or forgiveness offered by the Court system, and those who clutched The Good Book on oath are often the first to stand-up and condemn the accused. This point should be married to the fact that The Belsen Trials, in which Irma Grese was accused of war crimes, was undertaken by the British, with British judges and even a British Defence Counsel. This seems beyond belief on the point of bias, as Great Britain had spent almost six years combating a ferocious war with Germany and all those other axis forces who'd contributed in whatever way required to the Third Reich's war effort. Basically, despite best intentions and every legal protocol, it doesn't seem possible that a country who'd lost sons, daughters, husbands and wives (to name a few) and who harboured such hatred towards the Hitler regime could possibly be neutral in a case which carried the death sentence for those found guilty of alleged heinous crimes against humanity. Notwithstanding the language difficulties (translators were allowed) no German legal experts were permitted to prosecute or defend the accused. Maybe, given the circumstances, this is understandable, but why under the guidance of International Law and The League of Nations wasn't a neutral country (at the time of the war) such as Sweden or Switzerland given control of these trial proceedings? Surely, and it goes without saying, that the adoption of such a procedure would've been fairer on those being judged.

And then we must consider the question of revenge appertaining to those afflicted by Nazi brutality so close to the extinguished flames of conflict. But let's not make light of this because many of those giving evidence at the Belsen Trial had lost loved ones, not just a wife or husband, sister or brother; in many cases some were the sole survivors of a family dynasty which stretched as wide as second-cousins, back to great-grandparents and forward to pregnant women and the unborn, all of which had been obliterated by gas-chambers, starvation, disease or firing squads. On the reverse side of the coin however, what could be a better reason to exact revenge against those unlucky enough to be caught and consequently become the remnant representatives of the Nazi regime as a whole? Because some of those architects of the Final Solution and a few from the hierarchy of the Third Reich (and possibly Adolf himself [Hunting Hitler on TV's History Channel]) had each fled overseas, away from their pursuers like the panicked and scatter-brained mouse from the claws of a cat. So, it is possible, even most probably likely, that some of those standing trial were merely the scapegoats for those who were ultimately responsible for the holocaust; and we should not underestimate the storm-cloud of intolerant duress lower SS ranks (and their kin) were put under by their seniors, that threat of severe consequences for the slightest military offence such as dereliction of duty or disobedience of orders (like the vindictive headmaster with a cane.)

We know that there was much resentment and hatred towards the German people by the Jews at the end of the war. Because of the German defeat, the roles were suddenly reversed and they (the Germans) were now the hunted. Quite right too, but was the Sematic outrage perhaps bias by the magnitude and magnification of loathing engendered because of the Nazi crimes against them? Was there an extreme form of racism that existed at the time, a mirrored retribution exercised by Jews towards Germans? We only have to look at the revenge aftermath of a modern-day terrorist attack on our homeland to get the answer, our burgeoning intolerance to those who hold the same religion as the terrorists, all suddenly tarred with the same brush. And we should magnify the hatred that existed in the aftermath of Second World War because modern-day atrocities are on a much smaller and less enduring scale to those years of terror meted out by the gnarled fingers of the Third Reich to those she regarded as "enemies of the state."

"For the longest time I studied revenge to the exclusion of all else. I built my first torture chamber in the dark vaults of imagination. Lying on bloody sheets in the Healing Hall I discovered doors within my mind that I'd not found before, doors that even a child of nine knows should not be opened. Doors that never close again; I threw them wide." —Mark Lawrence

On the subject of revenge, I found the following interview interesting, recorded in "The Jerusalem Post" in 2012 and made by a holocaust survivor, a woman called Batsheva Dagan (formally Isabella Rubinstein) and a narrative relating specifically to Irma Grese:

"Back then I wanted to travel to Germany to testify, but the British, who ruled at the time, would not give me a travel certificate," she said. "So, The Palestine Post's editor found me and asked me to write for them."

She wrote the following:

"We, your victims, do not want you to die," read the letter addressed to Grese, which the newspaper ran in full on October 29, 1945. "We would much rather that you live, as we had to, with billows of filthy black smoke from the chimneys of the crematoria constantly before your eyes.

We want to see you dragging heavy stones, barefoot and in rags. We want to see you beaten, cruelly and mercilessly as you, cruel and without mercy, beat us. We want you to go so hungry that you cannot sleep at night, as we could not. We want to see your blonde hair shaved off, as you made us shave our heads."

Sixty-seven years later during her 2012 interview, she admitted the following:

"Such a letter I would not (today) be able to write and I'm amazed when I read it," said the diminutive woman in an interview held in the flower-filled living room of her apartment in Holon (a city on the central coastal strip of Israel, south of Tel Aviv). "Its main issue was revenge, revenge, revenge. It was a fire and brimstone piece, something I could not write today. Back then the urge for vengeance sought some release... nowadays I look for the human connection and I do not blame the younger generation for the sins of their parents or grandparents."

*

Research and literature on the subject of Irma Grese is almost entirely and exclusively one-sided with absolute condemnation of her guilt as a perpetrator of atrocious war crimes; it is also a time-consuming struggle for the impatient, pen-hovering story-teller! However, the evidential history is patchy due to the German destruction of records at Auschwitz and the British drastic 'up-in-flames' disease eradication of all the premises at Bergen-Belsen. Therefore, there is only word-of-mouth to rely upon, evidence of witnesses that is most likely tarnished by the previously mentioned revenge. Furthermore, the trial seemed rushed and inadequate. The best example of this is the case I attended recently as a Juror, the case against one individual (that mentioned earlier and relating to a far lesser charge than mass murder) which took seven days until a verdict was reached. There was not one but forty-five on trial at Luneburg; however, this ultimatum of legal proceedings (overshadowed by the death sentence) lasted from the 17th September until 17th November 1945, so just two months (or just over a day per defendant). Had the trial been given an adequate hearing and time-scale concerning the alleged crimes of the accused (prosecution, defence and deliberation by all concerned) then, based on the contemporary model I witnessed as a juror above, the trial would've lasted for over ten months of working weekdays. Lastly on this point, I would question the criminal investigations into the cases of each and every man and woman on trial in the Bergen-Belsen hearing at Luneburg. I know from the proceedings I attended that it took the police almost two years to investigate the case relating to just one accused individual. I accept that some might say that this's a parochial time-scale stuttered by the accused's availability, others that it's thorough. Nevertheless, it cannot be ignored that the investigations (if there were any) into forty-five alleged war-criminals prior to Luneburg was lackadaisical and inadequate because these lasted for only four months and were most likely founded on the hatred and say-so-revenge of individual complainants.

Now I'm not a lawyer but it strikes home that there's a further question in connection with the up-to-date (as of then) expertise legal methods of those judging, defending and prosecuting the Belsen cases of all concerned (the accused) after almost six years of frightful warfare. In the United Kingdom (the country's whose law was exercised at Luneburg) during the sixteenth century someone could have his or her head chopped off for stealing a chicken. But human-rights have moved on and evolved since then, through the ages where more and more crimes have become exempt from the hangman's noose, right up until the suspension of capital punishment in 1965. But things also accelerated along with technology; immediate decisions enabled by the telephone, the instant speed of the typewriter versus the lethargy of the printing press. But war delayed progress other than in weaponry advances and fighting finesse. The law of the land was one area of expertise that must've been put-on-ice, other than minor problems and those important issues that required Government intervention for the war-effort. This is because many of the law-makers, and those trained and employed to ensure compliance with such, were away and had enlisted in the Forces to fight for freedom from tyranny, where the judge fought alongside the dustman. And the postponement remained long after the conflict because those judges, barristers and solicitors who returned from the fight found their legal-beagle feet bogged down by the procrastination of bureaucrats who'd held fort while they were away, and also hugely depleted by the many souls of learned colleagues who'd fallen as casualties of war. So, what consequences did these delays have on the fate on those facing the death penalty at all war trials conducted by the United Kingdom? A huge amount is the answer, as in 1938 the issue of the abolition of capital punishment was brought before the British Parliament, one wrapped in bundles of bureaucracy and stuck together with lashings of red-tape. A clause within the Criminal Justice Bill called for an experimental five-year suspension of the death penalty. This was postponed when war broke out in 1939 and not enacted for another twenty-five years. Assuming haste (which is a bold assumption of politics) had it not been deferred and implemented as proposed, those executed at the Belsen Trials would've been exempt from such and therefore spared. Of course, most of them would've served time in goal but some may still have been alive today; one of those(at the time of writing my tale) was Irma Ida Ilse Grese.

Lastly there's guilt by association. If you watch the documentary called "The Accountant of Auschwitz," you will discover that the very old man on trial, Oskar Groening, was found guilty of war crimes, not because he'd ever murdered anyone but simply because he worked within the concentration camp's wicked system. It is compared to guarding the door to an office (in this case Oskar as look-out) while another ransacks and loots inside. Surely then, by the same measure of bias, the bombing and killing of innocents in the cities (both allied and enemy) should be regarded in the same light since the bomber crews knew of, but chose to ignore, the carnage they inflicted, like Oskar sitting at his desk in Auschwitz while remaining blinkered to the whirlwind of murder outside the paperwork.

Before I start on the trial of Irma (which I've tried to interpret from a different perspective than that usually written about) I'd like to throw into the mix the beguiling and hypnotic effect Adolf Hitler and his powerful rabble-rousing Nazi propaganda had upon some of the more gullible (more open-to-persuasion) members of German society prior to the outbreak of war (something I realise I've touched on before). Standing trial for crimes against humanity alongside Irma and the others was a fifty-two-year-old woman named

Juana Bormann, known in the death-camps as "The Woman with the Dogs." Her alleged cruelty in the process of the Final Solution was reported as unsurpassed by any other female guard; yet Juana had been raised with strict Christian faith and a cast-in-stone religious, Catholic creed, so much so that before enlisting in the SS she was a missionary who worked in a lunatic asylum and who spread the word of the Good Book in an unsurpassed altruistic manner to those patients housed within the refuge's screaming walls; Juana Bormann was an early victim of Hitler's Nazi brainwashing.

"The [Nazi] government will regard its first and supreme task to restore to the German people unity of mind and will. It will preserve and defend the foundations on which the strength of our nation rests... In place of our turbulent instincts, it will make national discipline govern our life." -Nazi proclamation to the German people, February 1933

*

The following are brief summaries by both the Prosecution and Defence teams prior to the Hearings appertaining to all those on trial for war-crimes:

Extract from "Law Reports of Trials of War Criminals," published 1947

"F. 'THE EVIDENCE FOR THE PROSECUTION

1. Brigadier H. L Glyn Hughes, e.B.E.,p.S.O., M.e.

Brigadier Glyn Hughes said that, shortly before the 15th April, 1945, certain German officers came to the headquarters of 8th Corps and asked for a truce in respect of Belsen camp. In pursuance of the arrangement arrived at, he went on the same day to Belsen camp, after it had been captured.

"There were piles of corpses lying all over the camp. Even within the huts there were numbers of bodies, some even in the same' bunks as the living. Most of the internees were suffering from some form of gastro-enteritis and were too weak to leave the huts. The lavatories in the huts had long been out of use. Those who were strong enough could get into the appropriate compounds but others performed their natural actions from where they were. The compounds were one mass of human excreta. Some of the huts had bunks, but not many, and they were filled absolutely to overflowing with prisoners in every state of

emaciation and disease. There was not room for them to lie down at full length in the huts. In the most crowded there were anything from 600 to 1,000 people in accommodation which should only have taken 100. There were large medical supplies in the stores at Belsen, but issues for the use of the prisoners were inadequate. The witness had made a tour of the camp accompanied by Kramer, the Commandant of Belsen; the latter seemed to be quite callous and indifferent to what they saw.

The principal causes of death in Belsen were lack of food and lack of washing facilities which in its turn led to lice and the spread of typhus."

PRELIMINARY OF DEFENCE:

"On behalf of all the accused it was argued that offences committed in concentration camps, even against prisoners of war, were not war crimes; that the offences alleged did not fall within the limited categories of war crimes which could be committed by civilians; that the victims were not always Allied nationals; that the concentration camp system was legal in German law, which was the system to which the accused owed their primary allegiance; that under German law many of the victims had become German subjects through the annexation of parts of Poland and Czechoslovakia; that it was incorrect to regard International Law as being dynamic in a sense which would allow a reversal of one of its principles; that the British Royal Warrant, Army Order 81/1945 as amended, did not set out to alter substantive International Law; that in general the State and not the individual was legally responsible for breaches of International Law; that the pre-April, 1944, text of paragraph 443 of the British Manual of Military Law (itself not a binding authority) was correct in law; and that it would be wrong to apply an amendment to that text made after the commission of many of the offences alleged. Counsel for individual accused argued that the affidavit evidence and much of the oral evidence before the Court was unreliable; that conditions or certain events in the camps were outside the control of the accused; that no prior agreement sufficient to make them jointly responsible under Regulation 8 (ii)* of the Royal Warrant had been shown; that Regulation 8 (ii)* could not be interpreted so as to make an accused liable for the acts of a superior or for offences of others more serious than those proved against the accused; that a certain degree of violence was necessary to keep order and to preserve food supplies; that the accused were protected even by the amended *text of paragraph 443 regarding superior orders; that it had not been proved that any of the persons named in the charge sheets as killed actually died at the hands of the accused; and that the Polish accused could not be regarded as war criminals."*

*(ii) Where there is evidence that a war crime has been the result of concerted action upon the part of a unit or group of men, then evidence given upon any charge relating to that crime against any member of such unit or group may be received as prima facie (accepted as correct unless proved otherwise) evidence of the responsibility of each member of that unit or group for that crime.

DAY 1

Irma Grese sat in the Courtroom dock in the front row of three pew-like tiered benches (each one rising towards the back) with several of the accused (male and female) sitting squashed together and uncomfortably along each bench, British, Canadian and American guards all around. She had the figure nine (for identification purposes) printed on a white card, strung inelegantly around her neck which rested cumbersomely on her breast; and she was sandwiched, shoulder-to-shoulder, between number eight (Herta Ehlert [female]) and number ten (Ilse Lithe [female]). Irma wore a blue suit (skirt and jacket) but her beautiful visage was impassive, showed nothing of the turmoil whirling around in her head; her blonde hair was swept back in an Ingrid Bergman styled quiff, golden ringlets bursting back from their hairband restraint, cascading down onto her slender shoulders like waves of silken tassels.

But the previous evening she'd heard the terrible news that Franz had passed away due to complications from typhus (no further details about exactly how or where he'd died were available due to translation difficulties). This had been told to her by Elisabeth via a reliable and non-malicious grapevine, commencing with an Englishman stationed at Bergen-Belsen and on through various gossip channels, ending up with the guard who paraded the corridor outside their cells. Aware of Irma's mood-swings from hope to despair, and despite the language barrier, Elisabeth had seized the opportunity to ask the guard about Franz's welfare, while out of her cell on an escorted visit to the washrooms, in the hope of heartening her friend's resolve with good news about his recovery. The news turned out to be simply awful, but something Elisabeth considered she couldn't hide from Irma.

When you lose love, you are suddenly bereft of reason and dazzled by grief, a hollowness that remains for a lifetime and the thereafter. It is life's malignant torture to fall in love, to find someone else who's faultless and perfect in every way and then lose them to a whim of vacuous suspicion or lust.

Love for another is something you carry in your heart, fold inside and caress daily even when it's gone, strayed away like some insular and introverted hobo. But those ghosts of hope remain to haunt and tease like a bully.

Franz's death was heart-breaking news for Grese whose frail sentiment still wobbled from her mother's suicide. What was the point of going on now Franz had passed away? She had little money; she hated her father so couldn't go home; her war of death and dying (of witnessing torture to humankind, gas-chambers, firing squads, rotting corpses; every kind of cruelty imaginable [and unimaginable] that lacerated her conscience) and this current courtroom ordeal had sapped any ambition or determination she'd once had; the last months (particularly the ruins of Berlin and Bergen-Belsen) years had sucked her life-force as if she'd been tossed into the swallowing quicksand's of despair; now she gulped a few last breaths before she sank because without Franz she'd rather be dead! Irma decided then and there not to make any feeble excuses in her defence and not bore the prosecutors with details of the mercy she'd offered, when she could, to those children (like Alice Tenenbaum) she'd saved from the gas-chambers; no absolutely not, preserve self-dignity and let the lashings from her horse-crop now turn on her, ready to take her penance and face a selection process with the weight of the Third Reich upon her shoulders. But the one thing she'd remembered as a child was her mother's hatred of the deceit that'd so often swaddled her father's slick denial of his many love affairs. It was that look-me-in-the-eye female intuition, a confirmation of truth her mother demanded but never found. Irma would not polish lies to enhance her court defence.

Richard Pope was with Irma, her reincarnated spirit as him (his pre-incarnate of her) had somehow stepped inside her being. No longer was he on that bus waving at her; for the first time his intellect realised and came to terms with his former self that'd been swallowed into her psyche. He saw through her eyes and felt her fear; was with her in the courtroom and could influence her thoughts in a positive, truthful and God-like manner. He seemed to breathe her every breath and now realised that he'd had been a woman in a previous life, an SS guard and one accused of war crimes. No more was she a nightmare to break from in anguish; now when she was in dreams, so was he; when she was awake and battling with conscience, so too was he. But the court hearing and consequent imprisonment, that would take several weeks from Irma's point of view, lasted only a few hours in the paroxysm of his subconscious.

A precis of some unlikely allegations made by plaintiff witnesses followed by my (the author's) critical comments:

Testifying Witnesses:

(1)

Dora Szafran

The witness had seen both Grese and Kramer beating internees. "Grese was one of the few S.S. women allowed to carry a gun. In Camp "A" in Block 9, two girls were selected for the gas chamber; they jumped from the window, and when they were lying on the ground Grese shot them twice."

The witness said that she was transferred to Belsen on 18th January, 1945. Here Grese had beaten a girl very severely.

Grese carried a pistol for self-defence and was not permitted to randomly shoot prisoners for whatever reason. Had she done so she would've faced severe consequences for disobedience. She might have been shot herself! The selection process was always taken outside (whatever the weather) and those chosen sent immediately to their fate. How can two girls jump from a window if they're outside? It just doesn't make sense. So, if this happened at all we can guess from Dora's statement that she was some distance from the grisly scene so most likely a case of mistaken identity as several female guards (blonde, blue-eyed Aryan types) looked similar to Irma.

(2)

Ilona Stein

Ilona Stein, a Jewess from Hungary, said that she was arrested on 8th June, 1944, and sent to Auschwitz. On 1st January, 1945, she was transferred to Belsen.

"At Auschwitz, Kramer, Grese and Mengele took part in selections: from the more experienced inmates she had learnt that the younger ones were taken to labour camps to work and the others to the crematorium. On one occasion some of the prisoners tried to hide. They were pointed out to the guard by Grese and they were shot. On another occasion a mother was talking to her daughter in another compound. Unfortunately, Grese saw her. She came on a cycle before the mother could get away and the mother was beaten severely and kicked by Grese." The witness had seen the accused often beating people in Auschwitz with a riding-whip. In an affidavit Stein said: *'At a selection a Hungarian woman tried to escape and join her daughter. Grese noticed this and ordered one of the S.S. guards to shoot the woman. I did not hear the order but I saw Grese speak to the guard and he shot at once. In Belsen, if Grese was taking roll-call and the count was not right, she made the prisoners stand for hours without food, even if it was cold, raining, or snowing. Even dying patients had to be brought out on these occasions.'*

It is not disputed that Irma Grese was, on occasions, extremely cruel to some prisoners; however, it is not proved that she ever committed a killing. In this statement she merely pointed out to a guard (or guards) those inmates who'd tried to hide from being taken to the crematorium (I assume she means selection.) All women guards were of lower rank to their male counterparts so couldn't order them to do anything; ergo his decision to shoot them. Unfortunately, their awful destiny had already been determined by the selection process and the guard was duty-bound to fulfil that order.

Now a section of Ilona's court testimony which is contradictory and doubtful and should've stricken from her evidence at the proceedings. Major Cranford was Irma's defence:

MAJOR CRANFIELD: (To the witness) Now let us turn to the beatings. Have you ever been beaten by Grese yourself?

THE WITNESS: I myself have been working in kitchen "C" from almost the very beginning and there Grese had not very great opportunity to beat me, but what I said I have seen about Grese beating others of them is true.

MAJOR CRANFIELD: The answer is "No"?

THE INTERPRETER: Yes.

THE WITNESS: I do remember now that once when a working party was out for work one member of this working party asked me some questions about relatives. When Grese saw that she jumped immediately and started beating me. That is an occasion which I do remember.

MAJOR CRANFIELD: (To the witness) Was the reason why you were beaten on that occasion because you were doing something you ought not to do?

THE WITNESS: As I mentioned before, it was not allowed to talk through the barbed wire and when this woman asked me about some relatives of hers, I answered and then Grese came immediately and started beating me.

Initially Ilona denies ever having been attacked by Irma Grese but then she suddenly changes her mind and recalls an incident of being the recipient of Irma's wrath. How could Ilona forget then swiftly recall such a severe incident that had happened in her recent history? This simply doesn't make sense; the mind is punctuated by pain (emotional and physical) and I can still vividly remember each punch and painful incident (mental and physical) I've ever received, some stretching back over forty years.

(3)

Helene Klein

"Grese "made sport" with the internees, making them fall down and get up for hours or crawl at an increasing speed. If anyone stopped, Grese beat them with a riding-whip she always had with her. The witness had been among the victims who were beaten."

We know this is probably true but almost certainly under the authority and orders of a senior Officer. Failure of SS staff to obey orders or deviate from duty would likely result in severe consequences for the offender.

Deponent's evidence by affidavit:

(1)

Gertrude Diament, a Jewess from Czechoslovakia, stated that during 1942 she had seen Volkenrath make selections; she would give orders that prisoners be loaded on to lorries and transported to the gas chamber. Grese was also responsible for selecting victims for the gas chambers at Auschwitz. Grese, at both Auschwitz and Belsen, when in charge of working parties, beat women with sticks and when they fell to the ground, she kicked them as hard as she could with her heavy boots. She frequently caused blood to flow and in the deponent's opinion many of the people she injured were likely to die from such injuries, but she had no direct evidence of such deaths.

It was strict camp policy that female guards did not have the authority to select victims for the gas chambers. While it is likely that they may have suggested certain persons for selection, the ultimate decision-making was the responsibility of the officer in charge. During this process, men were placed separately from women and children and an appointed officer of the Nazi party, typically an SS physician, would examine each of the deportees to determine whether they were in good physical health to be put to work; those who were not, typically the old and frail, to be exterminated.

(2)

143

Sonia Watinik, a Jewess from Poland, said that she saw Lothe, who was a kapo, beat her friend, Gryka, with her fists, making her nose bleed. . . . Watinik heard Lothe ask Grese to set her dog on Hanka Rosenzweig, and the dog bit the latter in the shoulder.

Although my little fictional story includes Khan, Irma's German Shepherd, we will learn later that two witness defendants (Hossler and Volkenrath) state that she never had a dog.

(3)

Defendant Helene Kopper said that she knew Schreirer as an Oberscharführer at Auschwitz in the winter of 1942-1943. She also saw him several times in Belsen. Grese was in charge of the Strafkommando (Punishment Kommando) working in a sand pit from 1942-1944. (In Court Kopper changed this period to seven months.) It was the practice of Grese to pick out certain of the Jewish woman prisoners and order them to get something from the other side of the wire. When the prisoners approached the wire, they were challenged by the guard, but as Grese usually picked out non-Germans they did not understand the order and walked on and were shot. She was responsible for at least 30 deaths a day resulting from her orders to cross the wire, but many more on occasions.

Thirty deaths a day and no one else noticed? Surely one of the other witnesses would've mentioned such an atrocity? Spurious allegations since she had an axe to grind against Irma and the whole Nazi regime she was imprisoned for loathing. Kopper was a Polish housewife and a political prisoner in the Auschwitz concentration camp (later Bergen-Belsen where she was a member of the camp police.) For almost the entire period of her imprisonment in Auschwitz, she was a member of the criminal squad because she violated the camp regulations (illegal possession of letters and cigarettes). So, this rule-breaker (and all of these type deviants are liars by nature) was placed in the penal command which was sternly led by overseer Irma Grese and would've undoubtedly led to Kopper's resentful and revenge-filled hatred of her charge.

While dealing with these points as above, we know that most inmates in concentration camps suffered from acute malnutrition and disease. This must've affected their memory (forgetfulness and uncertainty) to eye-witness events and to what extent might judgement have been impaired. Pertinent symptoms as follows:

Tiredness and irritability

An inability to concentrate

Depression

Feelings of depression, apathy and reductions in intellectual capacity are classical signs of Acute Malnutrition, particularly if these have progressed in recent weeks, and in parallel with signs of weakness or weight loss. These are usually obvious to the clinician during the examination and may coincide with lack of collaboration from the patient.

Transcripts from the hearing in defence of previous allegations made by plaintiff witnesses - 16th October 1945. Day twenty-six of the hearing (first of two concerning Irma).

The Official Shorthand Notes of 'The Trial of Josef Kramer and Forty-Four Others'

*Irma Grese. The accused, **IRMA GRESE** takes her stand at the place from which the other witnesses have given their evidence, and having been duly sworn is examined by MAJOR CRANFIELD as follows: Is your full name Irma Grese, and were you born on the 7th October, 1923? - **Yes.***

*You have heard what your sister said about your family; is that correct? - **Yes.***

*I want to take you to the time you left home. - **Yes.***

*Will you tell the Court what position you took and how long you were there? - **Yes ...***

COLONEL BACKHOUSE: Perhaps I might know what notes she is reading from.

THE PRESIDENT: Is she reading anything?

MAJOR CRANFIELD: She has copies of the affidavits against her in German; that is all.

*IRMA GRESE: **In 1938 I left the elementary school in Germany. It was customary to belong then afterwards either to the Arbeitsdienst (labour service) or to work for a year on the land in the country, agricultural work.***

MAJOR CRANFIELD: I want you to tell the Court what work you did and how long you stayed there. - I stayed there for six months on that farm and worked on agricultural jobs.

What work did you do after that and for how long? - **For six months in Luchen and worked there in a shop.**

And after that? - **When I was 15 I went to a hospital in Hohenluchen and stayed there for two years until I was 17.**

And after that? - **The sister there in that hospital tried to help me so that I should become myself also a nurse, but the labour exchange did not allow that and sent me to Fürstenberg to work there.**

What kind of work was that? - **In a dairy, working at a butter machine.**

And after that? - **In July, 1942, I was 18 then, I tried once more to become a nurse, but the Labour Exchange again sent me to Ravensbrück to a Concentration Camp.**

Had you any choice as to whether you joined the concentration camp service or not? - **No. I protested against it, but the Labour Exchange decided that I had to go.**

How long did you stay at Ravensbrück? - **March, 1943.**

Where did you go then? - **Auschwitz, Upper Silesia.**

Which camp in Auschwitz did you go to? - **Birkenau.**

How long did you stay in Auschwitz? - **To January, 1945.**

Now I want you to go through the whole period you were at Auschwitz and tell the Court the various duties which you did with the dates of the beginning and end of each one. Take it one by one. What was the first job you had in Auschwitz? - **Telephone duties in the Blockführer's (block leader's) room.**

Which camp in Birkenau was that? - **It was once A and once B camp; I changed over.**

What was the next job you had? - **For two days I was transferred as a sort of light punishment to be in charge of the Strafkommando (road construction detail) which carried** stones from outside into the camp. I received this punishment together with another Aufseherin because we did not wear our caps.

Was the accused Koper (Helene Kopper) in that strafkommando? - **I cannot remember.**

What happened after that? - **I do not remember whether I had Strassenbaukommando, kommando working on the roads, or gardening kommando; I am not sure about it.**

Can you remember the approximate date, the month, of the change? - **In Autumn, 1943.**

Did you ever at that time have the Strassenbaukommando? - **I am not sure whether it was Strassenbaukommando or the gardening kommando.**

That was not what I intended to ask. During 1943 did you at any time have the Strassenbaukommando? - **That was in the year of 1944 when I had the Strassenbaukommando.**

When you did have the Strassenbaukommando, for how long did you have it? - **No. I made a mistake; it was not 1944, it was 1943.**

When you did have it, whether it was 1943 or 1944, for how long did you have it? - **One to two weeks.**

During 1943, did you at any time have the gardening work party? - **Yes.**

For how long? - **One to two months.**

Can you remember the time of year when you had it; can you remember the months? - **It might have been in autumn.**

What job did you have after the gardening kommando? - **Post office, censoring mail.**

Which camp was that in? - **It was outside of the camp, compound A.**

Can you remember when that job began? - **Approximately in December, 1943.**

Can you remember when it ended? - **May, 1944.**

Where did you go then? - **Compound C.**

How long did you stay there? - **Till the end of December, 1944.**

What happened then? - **Then I was transferred for two weeks or two weeks and a half to Auschwitz No. 1.**

And after that? - **I left Auschwitz on the 18th January, 1945, and came to Ravensbrück.**

What was your job in Auschwitz No. 1? - **In charge of two blocks whose prisoners went to work during the day.**

Was it a women's camp you were in in Auschwitz No. 1? - **No, those two blocks were in the men's compound.**

Did you have any leave while you were at Auschwitz? - **Yes.**

When was that? - **It was in the beginning when I arrived. About June, I believe.**

To go back to Birkenau, were you ever in B Lager? - **There were several B camps in Birkenau; I do not know which one you mean.**

The women's camp I mean? - **There were two B camps; I do not know what you mean.**

Very well. When you left Auschwitz in January, 1945, where did you go to? - **Ravensbrück.**

And after that? - In March to Belsen.

Can you remember the date on which you arrived at Belsen? - **Beginning of March. I do not remember the day.**

MAJOR CRANFIELD: You told us this morning that you were in charge of the Strassenbaukommando for a period of one or two weeks. Do you remember whether the accused Koper was in that Kommando or not? - **No, I am quite sure she has not been there.**

Was that kommando a punishment kommando? - **Yes, it was a punishment kommando but it last [lost] the title punishment kommando and was called Strassenbaukommando.**

You also told us that for two days you were in charge of another strafkommando carrying stones? - **Yes.**

Apart from these two occasions were you at any time at Auschwitz in charge of any other punishment Kommando? - **No.**

Were you at any time at Auschwitz in the parcels office? - **In the post censorship department.**

I want to know about the parcels office. - **Volkenrath was really in charge of the parcels office, but for two or three days she had been sent away and I took over during that time.**

Can you remember the month and the year that was? - **1943; I do not know in which month.**

I want to ask you about the time you were in "C" lager. Were there any other Aufseherinnen there? - **Another six or seven.**

Were the other Aufseherinnen there during the whole time you were there? - **The others were changed every week.**

Were you senior to them? - **Yes.**

How many blocks were there in "C" Lager? - **There were 28 blocks where prisoners were accommodated, then there was one block for food, food stores, one office, company office, two stores with underwear and clothing, two or three blocks for latrines and two washhouses.**

How many prisoners were there? - **Approximately 30000.**

What nationality were they? - **All Hungarians and the Blockältesten (block elders) they were Czechoslovaks.**

Was there always the same number of prisoners or did it change? - **No, that was the highest number, 30000, but I generally had about 20000.**

Did the prisoners stay there the whole time you were there or did they come and go? - **They came and went.**

When prisoners came to you in "C" lager what was the procedure on their arrival? - **When the transports arrived, they had been already selected and those who arrived were found** *fit for work. When they arrived, they went into the washhouse, they washed there and then they had their hair cut and then they were distributed.*

You have told us that the number of prisoners varied between 20000 and 30000. When the numbers of prisoners went up did the number of Aufseherinnen go up? - **No.**

You have told us that there were 28 living huts. How many prisoners could they properly accommodate? - **The normal accommodation would have been for a hundred or perhaps two hundred or let us say a maximum of three hundred, but I had to take in 1000 for each block because the camp was overcrowded.**

In these blocks were there any beds? - **No, in some of the blocks there were some sort of bunks which were big enough for five people, so that five could sleep on one bunk, but in most of the blocks there were neither beds nor bunks.**

How did the prisoners behave? - **In the beginning when there were smaller numbers of them and they had sufficient to eat they were quite all right; later on, when I had 20000 of them, 25000 and 30000 then they behaved like animals.**

How did they behave when the food was being distributed? - **As I said before, in the beginning it was quite all right; later on when food was a bit more scarce then at food distribution when people carried the food from the kitchen to the blocks nearly at every corner there were 20 or 30 people who waited to pounce upon them and to take the food away.**

We have heard something about sanitary conditions. How did the prisoners behave in regard to latrines? - **In the beginning it was quite all right; later on when the camp was overcrowded then wherever you went it was just as if the prisoners thought that any place is good enough for a latrine and they just defecated wherever they stood or wherever they went and those proper latrines they were ruined by throwing all sorts of stuff into them until they simply ceased to function.**

How old were you at this time when you were in "C" Lager? - **20.**

I want to ask you about allegations of ill-treating the prisoners. Did you carry a stick at Auschwitz? - **In camp "C", yes.**

What kind of a stick was it? - **It was a simple walking stick.**

Did you carry a whip at Auschwitz? - **Yes**

What kind of whip was it? - **It was made in the weaving factory in the camp out of cellophane.**

MAJOR CRANFIED: We have heard of the whips made in the weaving factory before and the Court wants to know what kind of a whip it was. Will you describe to the Court the appearance of it and the size of it? - **This length (Indicating). There were three parts and each part was that size.**

Can you give the Court some indication of whether it was a heavy whip or not? - **No, it was a very light whip.**

If you hit somebody with it would it hurt? - **Oh yes.**

If it had not hurt it would have not been much use to you, would it? - **Yes, of course that is what I said.**

Did you ever at Auschwitz carry a rubber truncheon? - **No.**

While we are on this subject of weapons, I want to ask you this. Did you carry a stick at Belsen? - **No.**

Did you at Belsen carry any kind of weapon? - **No.**

Now I want to go back for a moment to the whips made in the weaving factory. What happened to those? - **We had those whips for eight days or for a fortnight and then the Kommandant, Kramer, prohibited them, but we nevertheless went on using them.**

Now I want you to explain to the Court the occasions on which you struck the prisoners with your stick or your whip and why you did so - **In the beginning I did not use anything at all. Later on when the crowds in Camp "C" became bigger and bigger then a sort of general stealing started; very much was stolen. It was so with the whole camp that the prisoners did not obey any orders. I gave orders, quite light orders, and even those were not obeyed. Every day, for instance, two Aufseherinnen who were working in the kitchen came complaining that again things have been stolen, again margarine had disappeared. I** *could not know, of course, who were the thieves so therefore I put two Aufseherinnen in charge and I gave them orders to keep their eyes open and whenever they found somebody on the spot who stole something to give them a good thrashing. In the beginning every prisoner had two blankets but later of course when the crowds became bigger, I had to see to it that everybody got a blanket and therefore each prisoner only got one blanket. We had about 30000 blankets in camp "C" but then later on when one day we wanted to see how many there were I found out that only half the number was available. I, of course, was responsible for them. I had to go and account where the others had gone.*

*What I want you to explain to the Court is on what occasions you struck prisoners and the reasons why you did it. Do not be too long winded about it. - **That is what I am telling you. We found they had cut up all these blankets and made all sorts of things out of them; they made shoes, little jackets, all sorts of clothing, even small carpets for their beds - something like that - and I gave strictest orders that all these things which had been made out of blankets had to be returned at once. In spite of my strict orders the result was nothing. I did not get anything at all, so then I ordered the control of all the blocks and also personal searches of the prisoners. On those occasions I used my whip. For instance, parades, the Jewish Lagerälteste (elders) gave the signal for parades. In half an hour the whole camp should have been on parade. Still there were always prisoners who tried to evade it, who tried to hide themselves under the bed or even in wardrobes, wherever they could. When my other Aufseherinnen reported to me the numbers and I compared them and they were not all right then, of course, I gave them orders. I gave orders to the Aufseherinnen to count again and again until these two or three who were missing would be found and therefore because of these few who tried to hide themselves sometimes parades took three or four hours. As I was responsible for the camp, I said the parades would go on until the number was all right.***

*Have you ever taken an individual prisoner and beaten her until she fell to the ground senseless? - **No***

*Have you ever taken an individual prisoner and beaten her until she was bleeding? - **No.***

*Have you ever kicked a prisoner whom you have struck to the ground? - **Never.***

152

At Belsen have you ever struck a prisoner at all? - **Yes.**

With what? - **With the hand.**

Have you at Belsen ever struck a prisoner with anything other than your hand? - **No.**

What was the condition of the prisoners at Belsen? - **The condition of the prisoners were so bad that one had almost a horror of them.**

Do you remember an SS woman called Buckhalla [Buchhalter]? - **Yes.**

You heard Volkenrath describe the occasion on which she was punished. Was the description correct? - **Yes.**

Were you present? - **Yes.**

Did the Kommandant, Hoess, give you an order on that occasion? - **Yes.**

What was that? - **I had the order that the last two out of the 25 strokes with which she was punished by Reichsführer Himmler that I myself should give her the last two of these.**

How old were you when that happened? - **20.**

I want to ask you about Appell parades (role call). What was the signal for the prisoners to get on parade? - **It was a blow on a special whistle.**

Who had the whistle? - **It was different; sometimes the Aufseherin, sometimes the Lagerälteste, sometimes the Kapo (prisoners appointed to help the SS).**

When you were in "C" Lager where did the orders come from for a parade? - **For the roll call, for counting purposes, it was me who gave the orders.**

Where did the order come from for what we call selection parades? - **That came by telephone from a Rapportführerin or from Oberaufseherin (head overseer) Dreschel.**

When the order came were you told what the parade was for? - **No.**

What were the prisoners supposed to do when the whistle went? - **Fall in in fives.**

What were the duties then of yourself and the other Aufseherinnen? - **To see to it that they fell in in fives.**

When they were fallen in what were your duties then? - **Then came Dr. Mengele and made the selection.**

What were your duties while Dr. Mengele made the selection? - **As I was responsible for the camp my duties were to know how many were leaving my camp and I had to count them.**

Did you keep a strength book? - **Yes.**

After a selection what did you enter in your strength book? - **After the selection took place they were sent then into "B" Camp and then afterwards a telephone call came from Oberaufseherin Dreschel who told me either that they went to another camp in Germany for working purposes or that they went into the gas chamber. She did not say exactly gas chamber. She said S.B., special treatment, so therefore I thought special treatment is equivalent to gas chamber. Then I put it in my strength book either so many for transfer to Germany to another camp and so many for S.B., special treatment.**

How did you learn that S.B meant the gas chamber? - **That was well known to the whole camp.**

Were you ever told anything about the gas chamber by your senior officers? - **No.**

Who was it then who told you about the gas chamber? - **The prisoners told me about it.**

You have been accused of choosing prisoners on these parades and sending them to the gas chamber; have you done that? - **No.**

At the time when these parades took place in Auschwitz had you any knowledge of the gas chamber apart from what the prisoners told you? - **I knew that prisoners were gassed there.**

Did you carry a pistol at Auschwitz? - **In Camp "C" yes.**

Why was that? - **It was rather dangerous in the last months to be without a pistol because of the partisans, and I carried it only for self-protection.**

Was your pistol loaded? - **No.**

Did you carry a pistol at Belsen? - **No.**

Have you ever fired your pistol at a prisoner? - **No.**

Have you ever fired a pistol at all? - **No - oh yes, on New Year's Eve.**

What did you fire at then? - **Into the air. It was not a revolver; it was a sort of hunting rifle.**

At Auschwitz did you ever have a dog? - **No.**

Were there dogs there? - **Yes.**

What kind of dogs were they? - **I do not know exactly what sort of dogs, but they were trained dogs.**

Did you ever have anything to do with them? - **No.**

I want to go back to Appell for a moment. Did you ever order prisoners to kneel down at an Appell? - **[Yes].**

Why was that? - **Because we could not properly count; they were running to and fro.**

MAJOR CRANFIELD: I am now going to put to the witness the specific accusations against her. I will start off with the witness Szafran, volume 7 of the transcript. (To the witness) A witness accused you of beating a girl at Belsen with a riding crop about a fortnight before the British troops arrived. Is that true? - **No.**

The same witness said that you came to her kitchen on an inspection with Kramer. Is that true? - **I never went on an inspection with Kramer.**

During the time you were at Belsen what were your duties? - **I was Arbeitsdienstführerin responsible for working parties.**

Will you explain to the Court what the duties of an Arbeitsdienstführerin were? - **The Arbeitsdienstführerin is responsible for all the outside working kommandos. She has to be** *there when they leave the camp and distribute working tickets for the respective kommandos.*

The same witness said that at Auschwitz at a selection at which Blockälteste Rehr, the accused Hössler and Dr. Enna were present, two girls jumped out of the window and you shot them while they were lying on the ground. Is that true? - **In camp "C" neither Hössler nor Dr. Enna nor Blockälteste Rehr were ever present on selections. It must have been in camp A.**

THE JUDGE ADVOCATE: That is what the witness said. The evidence was that a selection took place in Camp A block 9.

MAJOR CRANFIELD: Yes, I think I said Auschwitz. The witness is saying "C" lager because the greater part of her time was in that camp.

THE JUDGE ADVOCATE: But she is saying if that occurred it would be in Camp A. That is what Szafran said. Will you clear it up?

MAJOR CRANFIELD: Yes. (To the witness) Did you ever shoot two girls under those circumstances? - **I never at or never shot at all at any prisoner.**

MAJOR CRANFIELD: The next one is the witness Stein, whose evidence appears in volume 9 on pages 12 to 16. (To the witness) That witness told us that at a selection in the summer of 1944 some prisoners tried to hide, but that you saw it, told somebody, and a woman was shot. Is that true? - **I cannot remember.**

It was suggested that the woman was shot by an SS man on guard. - **I do not remember.**

THE JUDGE ADVOCATE: Which incident is this?

MAJOR CRANFIELD: This is the incident of the Hungarian woman. There were two incidents concerning Stein; this is the woman who was hiding from a selection parade and she turned out to be Hungarian. I think that came out in answer to a question put by me. It is the first of the two Stein incidents. (To the witness) Had you any authority to issue orders to an SS guard? - **No.**

THE JUDGE ADVOCATE: Are you sure it was given in evidence and not in an affidavit?

MAJOR CRANFIELD: Yes; it is in volume 9 of the transcript, page 14 at the top.

THE JUDGE ADVOCATE: I think, Sir, with great respect, I do not want to be hurried over this, and I want to be corrected if I am wrong. I have taken a note of what the witness said as distinct from what was said in the two depositions, and I have got against Stein an incident where the first is an allegation that Grese made them stand before their block in all weathers naked. The second one is to be found in the transcript: I saw from a window in the kitchen some people trying to hide. Grese saw this and told someone else and they were shot. This was about the end of August 1944. I helped to collect those shot, put them in a blanket and took them away. Is that the one you are talking about?

MAJOR CRANFIELD: Yes.

THE JUDGE ADVOCATE: Then surely the Hungarian woman is the next one?

MAJOR CRANFIELD: No, I think you will find in cross examination I got the answer that that woman was a Hungarian.

THE JUDGE ADVOCATE: If you are talking about that incident, I am quite clear, but I did not understand the point about the SS men and the shooting which was in the affidavit but which was not brought out here.

MAJOR CRANFIELD: The same witness alleged there was an incident when a mother was talking to her daughter over the wire between two compounds. (To the witness) It is alleged that you arrived on a bicycle and beat the mother so severely that she was lying on the ground where you kicked her; is that true? - **I do not deny that I beat her, but I did not beat her until she fell to the ground, and I did not kick her either. That is a lie.**

At Auschwitz did you wear a belt with your uniform? - **No. I wore the belt with the pistol together.**

Will you look at this and say whether this is the one you wore? - **(Same handed) Yes.**

Did you ever at Auschwitz wear any other kind of belt? - **No.**

MAJOR CRANFIED: I would like to put this belt in as an exhibit.

(Belt is marked Exhibit "126", signed by the President and attached to the proceedings)

MAJOR CRANFIELD: I did not propose to put anything else out of Stein's evidence, as I think it has all been covered by the general questions on selections, beatings, and so forth.

THE JUDGE ADVOCATE: That is entirely a matter for you, because Stein is not taking the same view that the accused did. She says "We had to stand before the blocks naked in all weathers". I do not know how far you want to go into it.

MAJOR CRANFIELD: I do not propose to go into that. The next witness is Rozenwayg, volume 10 page 17 of the transcript. (To the witness) The witness accused you of setting your dog on to her when you were on a Kommando with the accused Lothe at Auschwitz? - **I have never been with Lothe on an outside working party. Secondly, I never had a dog.**

MAJOR CRANFIELD: I am not [now] going on to the affidavits. The first one is 22, exhibit 26. (To the witness) Take your German translations and open them at page 22. Do you see in the affidavit that Dunklemann describes you as aged about 30, blond, with hair tied up at the back? - **Yes.**

Just look at the hair of No. 7 (indicating Volkenrath). - **Yes.**

Is the hair style of Volkenrath known in Germany as having your hair tied up at the back? - **It is called in Germany something like "All Clear", because everything goes up so it is "All Clear".**

MAJOR CRANFIELD: I am now going on to affidavit 113, exhibit 66; the deponent Neiger. (To the witness) Do you see in that affidavit it is alleged that Appelle were from 0300 hours to 0900 hours? - **Yes.**

At Auschwitz what was the light at 0300 hours? - **Very dark. I never got up at 3 o'clock.**

Do you see that the deponent says that there were 31000 people in camp "C", and that you ordered them to hold their hands above their heads with a large stone in each? - **Yes.**

COLONEL BACKHOUSE: I do not want to interrupt my friend, but from a fair reading of that affidavit it obviously does not suggest that all the internees had to do it. It is quite obvious what she was talking about.

MAJOR CRANFIELD: (To the witness) Did you ever order the prisoners in your charge to stand holding a large stone above their heads in each hand? - **No; I must add that Katherine Neiger was not a second in my camp at all, and has never been in my camp.**

Were there any large stones in Camp "C" available for such a purpose? - **That is the size of the stone (Demonstrating).**

MAJOR CRANFIELD: The next one is page 160 of the summary, exhibit 87. (To the witness) Do you see in that affidavit an accusation that you shot a Hungarian Jewess outside one of the blocks during the arrival of a transport. Is that true? - **Yes, I have seen it.**

Is that true? - **I do not deny that the woman had been shot, but I do deny that she was shot by me.**

How did the shooting happen? - **I do not remember the incident with this woman. I do not know whether it is the same incident, but I remember in Camp "C" that happened also during the arrival of a transport; a woman was shot by a guard from a watch tower, but whether it is the same woman I cannot say.**

Will you read the second accusation which is in paragraph 4 of that affidavit? - (After reading paragraph) Yes.

Is that true? - **No. I must state that all this is terribly exaggerated. I might have taken one woman out who did not stay in her place and put her into another row, and I might have slapped her face, but that I beat her savagely until she was bleeding is a total lie.**

MAJOR CRANFIELD: The next one is exhibit 88, page 163. (To the witness) Will you read paragraph 2 of the affidavit? - **(After reading paragraph) Yes.**

Is that true? - **I did not have a dog. I do not remember that working party, but I had a bicycle. Then it says that I had something to do with Block 25. I have never been there. I was only there once.**

MAJOR CRANFIELD: My interpreter says the answer was that she had never been in block 25 at all.

THE PRESIDENT (To the Interpreter): What was the answer?

THE INTERPRETER: "I have never been there, not once". I misunderstood her.

MAJOR CRANFIELD: The next affidavit is No. 169, exhibit 90. Will you read paragraph 4? - *(After reading paragraph) Yes*.

This incident which is described by three people, two of whom were witnesses, and one an affidavit...

THE JUDGE ADVOCATE: Has it been put in as an exhibit?

MAJOR CRANFIELD: I was under that impression. It is in volume 16 and is at page 45.

The next one is the statement of the accused Koper.

THE PRESIDENT: We have not had an answer to this yet.

MAJOR CRANFIELD: I beg your pardon. (To the witness) Is the incident described in paragraph 4 of that affidavit true? - *No.*

The next one is the statement of the accused Helene Koper, page 46, exhibit 110...

THE JUDGE ADVOCATE: The trouble is you go so quickly. I have got this incident entered up against Lothe.

MAJOR CRANFIELD: Also against Lothe.

THE JUDGE ADVOCATE: The exhibit was probably produced as some evidence against Lothe, but I have now got my note in order, so it is all right to go on.

MAJOR CRANFIELD: We have had an answer. (To the witness) The next one is 46, statement of Helene Koper, exhibit 110. Will you look at the statement, paragraph 2 and paragraph 3. Is that true? - It is possible that Helene Koper had an incident like this with some Aufseherin, but certainly not with an Aufseherin Irma Grese.

Have you at Auschwitz ever been in charge of a Kommando working in a sand pit? - *No.*

Have you ever sent prisoners to cross a wire in order to be shot? - *Never.*

MAJOR CRANFIELD: Now those are all the specific instances which I was going to put to the accused. I think all the others are covered by the general denials. Unless there is anything else which the Court wish me to put?

THE JUDGE ADVCATE: Major Cranfield, a member of the Court would like you, if you would, to deal with the evidence of Sunschein, where she made an allegation that a kommando received some sort of general punishment from Grese of having to run about for half an hour. The member would like you to deal with the collective punishment at their work.

MAJOR CRANFIELD: Yes, I will. I will go to Belsen now, I have one or two general questions about Belsen. I will go there now and deal with that, if I may, after.

THE JUDGE ADVOCATE: That is a Belsen allegation?

*MAJOR CRANFIELD: Yes. (To the witness) I want to ask you about the camp at Belsen. I want you tell the Court what the conditions at Belsen were like when you arrived there at the beginning of March this year and how they were between then and the arrival of the British? - **Almost daily transports arrived and the camp was very much overcrowded.***

*You have told us that you had a horror of the prisoners? - **Yes, I was horrified because the prisoners were so dirty and so ill.***

*What effect did that have on your work there? - **I do not quite understand the question.***

*You have told us that you were the Arbeitsdienstführerin; you have told us that the camp was very overcrowded, always becoming more overcrowded; you have told us that the prisoners were so dirty and so ill that you had a horror of them. What I want to know is how did those conditions affect you in the work you had to do? - **I had to attend the roll call twice a week, and every time I came back from the camp I felt horrified.***

*One of the witnesses who came here told of you "making sport " with a Kommando for half an hour. Do you remember that incident? - **Yes.***

*If that is true? - **Yes.***

*Can you remember why you did that? - **I was in my office and looked out of the window. I saw a group of kitchen workers coming back and they were stopped by Aufseherin. I saw that behind this kommando something was thrown away, it was two parcels wrapped in paper. I went to have a look at these parcels and I saw that each of them consisted of at least two pounds of meat from the kitchen. We asked several times who had thrown this away but nobody told us. I promised the Kommando that I would not report them or do any harm to them if I was told who had thrown these parcels away. They all kept silent and then I said, "Well then we have to make sport until the person who has thrown these parcels away tells us about it." We made sport for about half an hour and then some of the prisoners told us who had thrown these parcels away. I had promised the kommando not to report this incident and so I did not do it; I thought they had been punished enough by this sport.***

*It was alleged that those who were not doing it properly were beaten by you with a riding crop; is that true? - **Their sport was being made very well. In the second place I had no riding whip, and I had not been beating them.***

*Had you done this kind of collective punishment before? - **No, I only had seen it.***

*Are extra parades and extra drills a recognised form of punishment in the German service? - **Yes, you can say that.***

*Now in this case you are accused of being concerned together with Kramer and Klein and Hössler, both at Auschwitz and Belsen. I want to ask you first of all about Auschwitz. Have you ever planned with Kramer in regard to sending prisoners to the gas chamber? - **No.***

*Have you ever planned with Klein or Hössler? - **No.***

*Has any one of those three ever consulted you with regard to who was to go to the gas chamber? - **We have never been talking about these things. Kramer, Klein and Hössler were my superior officers. If Kramer came into the camp, I had to make out my report, as was my duty, and nothing else.***

*Have you ever planned with Kramer or any other of the accused to deliberately ill-treat a prisoner at Auschwitz? - **No.***

*Have you ever planned with them the death or deliberate ill-treatment of a prisoner at Belsen? - **Never.***

*I want to ask you about the film which we saw. Did you observe in that film that at one moment there was thick snow on the ground and at the next moment there was none at all? - **Yes.***

MAJOR CRANFIELD: That is all I have to ask.

*Cross-examined by CAPTAIN PHILLIPS: Do you know the numbers of the cookhouses at Belsen? - **Yes.***

*Whereabouts in the camp was No. 1? - **In the men's camp.***

THE PRESIDENT: Who is this?

*CAPTAIN PHILLIPS: This is directed to all my four accused. (To the witness) And No. 2? - **No. 2 also.***

*CAPTAIN PHILLIPS: I think you will find this of interest to quite a number of accused. No. 1 is in the men's camp and No. 2 is in the men's camp. (To the witness) Are No. 3 and No. 4 in the women's camp? - **Yes.***

*Where is No. 5? - **No. 3 was sub divided in two parts, but both were called No. 3. No. 5 was not No. 5 but No. 4.***

CAPTAIN PHILLIPS: I do not know whether I may explain what I understood the witness to say. No. 3 cookhouse is divided into two parts, which is No. 3 and No. 4.

*THE PRESIDENT: Where is No. 5? - **Both parts of No. 3, although sub divided, have still the No. 3, and No. 5 does not exist at all, it is No. 4. Altogether there are five kitchens.***

*But there is 3A and 3B, both called No. 3? - **Yes.***

*CAPTAIN PHILLIPS: Do you know in which kitchen No. 38 worked (Frieda Walter)? - **Number 3.***

*Will No. 37 stand up? (The accused Herta Bothe stands up) - **No. 37 was in charge of the distribution of wood.***

*Will No. 39 stand up. (The accused Irene Haschke stands up) - **She was in one part of Kitchen No. 3. That is the kitchen which was divided; I do not know in which part of kitchen No. 3 she was working.***

*Cross-examined by LT JEDRZEJOWICZ: You said there was an Oberaufseherin Dreschel in Auschwitz. Was she the Aufseherin who was in charge of the whole women's camp? - **Yes.***

*Was she a severe woman? - **Very severe.***

*Were the prisoners and Blockältesten and Lagerältesten afraid of her in the same way? - **Yes, in the same way.***

*Now a question about Belsen camp. Who was in a position to withhold food in Belsen Camp as a punishment? - The **Kommandant.***

*Are you quite sure that a Blockälteste or a Lagerälteste was not in a position, had no right, no power whatever, to withhold food as a punishment for his block or Lager? - **Yes.***

*

Fifty Second Day - Thursday, 15th November, 1945

The Judge Advocate's summing up of the evidence for and against Irma Grese. Further points of conflicting and unsafe evidence.

Evidence from Franz Hossler (SS second lieutenant [male])

"I saw Grese and her work in Auschwitz. She worked in my camp and she did not have a dog. As an overseer she worked in the post office. At night she had to help Blockführerinnen on their Appelle. She had to censor mail. I saw how she worked on Appelle and she was very good and very efficient. I was Grese's Lagerführer (camp leader). Grese is capable of loading and firing a pistol."

Evidence from Elisabeth Volkenrath (Lead SS female guard)

"I know Grese. Our duties lay together at Auschwitz and I served with her at Belsen for a few weeks. At Auschwitz and Belsen she served under me. I never saw her with a dog."

Evidence from Rosenwayg (Jewish Prisoner)

"In June, 1943, Lothe (Ilse Lothe German political prisoner and Kapo) complained to Grese of my work and I was bitten by Grese's dog. I had to go on working to escape going to hospital and the gas chamber."

16th November. Major Cranfield's plea of mitigation for Irma Grese

MAJOR CRANFIELD: I have nothing fresh with regard to my two accused who remain, and I have only to recall to your mind what you have already heard.

With regard to Grese, you will remember that she told you her mother died when she was 14 years of age, and she herself left her home at the age of 16, and at the age of 18 she was conscripted into the concentration camp service. You have heard from Starostka of the difficulties which she encountered in controlling the women under her when she first went into a concentration camp. There can, I think, be no doubt that among these women there were many of a low and brutal type, and Grese was a girl of only eighteen years when she first had to face up to it. A year later she came to the appalling atmosphere of Auschwitz. I would remind you of a phrase which I think is most significant. It was used by the Polish witness Komsta in connection with Hössler. She said: "He was a master of our life and death and we were terrified of him." I invite the Court to consider the terrible atmosphere there must have been at Auschwitz where a word or a movement either way meant death. It was to that atmosphere that Grese was sent at the age of nineteen.

Again I would remind you of the incident when all the Aufseherinnen were paraded and where one was flogged after the Kommandant had read out the sentence which came from Himmler, and how this Kommandant turned to Grese, a girl of twenty, and ordered her to add two further strokes to the victim. I ask you to consider that incident. This young girl

receiving an order of that kind from a man who was a Colonel in the SS. She was less than a
private soldier, aged twenty, and I would ask you to consider what sort of effect that must
have had upon her.

A large part of the charge at Auschwitz against her arises in regard to Camp "C", and
again I would recall to you mind her position there. Under her she had 30000 Hungarian
women, and to help her only six other Aufseherinnen. She, a girl aged twenty.

Lastly, in regard to Grese, I would remind you that she is only a poorly educated girl. Her
father was an agricultural labourer and she was a subject of the Nazi propaganda machine. I
ask you to consider how far what she has done has been done of her own free will.

17th November 1945. Day fifty-four of proceedings.

Sentencing.

THE PRESIDENT: No. 6 Bormann, No. 7 Volkenrath, No. 9 Grese. The sentences of this
Court, on each of you whom I have just named, is that you suffer death by being hanged.

The initial effect of the judge's stun-shocked words in Irma Grese's (and Richard Pope's)
intellect was like a sting from the fangs of the cobra; it exploded in her reasoning like a
hydrogen bomb. She looked composed but inwardly felt a shudder as cold as a shard of ice
stab her heart and puncture her hitherto confidence that she'd only receive a minor
sentence; that sinking feeling of utter despair, suddenly gutted of the absorption of hope
befalling the condemned. The Jews had lied and she now had to face the consequences of
their collective guile, mistruths and their contrived deception spat from spiteful tongues.
The only slight consolation she felt was that in death she'd be reunited with Franz and her
mother, that unbiased and comforting warmth of wanting.

A subsequent appeal for clemency to Field Marshall Bernard Montgomery (British
Commander) was rejected. This is no surprise as Monty had forged a career as a soldier and
therefore sculptured a granite psyche at bedfellows with the merciless death and
destruction of others.

"This is the way the world ends. Not with a bang but a whimper." — T.S. Eliot

CHAPTER 15 (and epilogue)

The following day Irma Grese was transported to Hamelin goal to await the awful and final execution of her sentence. She travelled with Elisabeth Volkenrath and Juana Bormann both of whom had also received the death penalty.

It's dreadful to await death when healthily fully conscious and in unrestrained vigour without the reason of compassionate release from pain or disease. Irma would rather have been surprised by a bullet to the head than suffer the waiting process for the gross indignity of being hanged. But she didn't have long to wait, only twenty-six days as Montgomery's Death Warrant was issued on 7th December 1945.

Irma's letter of 29 November 1945 written from prison to her sister, Helene Grese:

Leni! My dear little sister!

You have made me very happy with the good news from home. I am quite another person. Now we must cross our fingers that I can stay alive. I am not letting my courage sink, and I hope that a little change will come into view.

*Leni! Is it true that my Anneli has left something good for me? [*Note: Anneli was a girl courtroom-observer who became particularly interested in Irma Grese and took up written correspondence with her via Helene Grese. She apparently wanted to procure poison for Irma to enable the dignity of suicide.] This was my only wish, to get something like that so as not to be hanged like a witch! Now I am quite at ease, for now I know that I can avoid the terrible manner of death by making an easy end to myself. Leni, please send best wishes to my Anneli and many, many thanks for her sports event (as in sporting or helpful attitude), which has come to me as if on demand! If I should no longer be in a position to thank Annelies, you will have to look after it, for she is my saviour - ! (You know what I mean, don't you)? Just imagine, Leni! Anneli likes me so much, she is putting her own life on the line just to free me from the fear of death. She is quite simply rescuing me from the terrible fate that is facing me. I can't find words of thanks, for it is the greatest happiness granted to me in the last days of my life! That happiness is: a sports event from my dear Anneli!*

Don't have any bad thoughts, for I am still a little hopeful!! - If it really must be, and I am to do, don't you be sad, for I am dying for my country! You have to be as proud of that as I am! I can still hope and not let myself be robbed of hope! ----- If I have other thoughts, I will write to Anneli too, since she deserves it!

Kisses from

Irmkins.

Regards to Anneli.

On the 13th December 1945 at 10.03 in the morning, Irma Ida Ilse Grese was hung for war crimes on a gallows scaffold erected by the British Royal Engineers following the specific design of the hangman. Her neck snapped like a twig to the dull twang of the tensed noose.

At 10.03 in the morning of the 13th December 2014 Richard Pope's eyes sprang open from a brain-seize hypnotic trance. He bolted upright from his seat like a jack-in-the-box, looking agasp and bewildered, his face gaunt with a blast of confusion. He eager-eyed across the table from the confines of Tony Ludlow's therapy room and said to the psychiatrist, 'Excuse me, but where am I; and who on Earth are you?'

Richard's nightmare was at an amnesia-to-Irma end.

Irma Grese's executioner was a British man by the name of Albert Pierrepoint, a foul and loathsome person of low morals and candour. At the time of her execution, he was forty years old. In his biography, he describes the events leading up to Irma's hanging as follows:

"At last, we finished noting the details of the men, and RSM O'Neil ordered 'bring out Irma Grese'. She walked out of her cell and came towards us laughing. She seemed as bonny a girl as one could ever wish to meet. She answered O'Neil's questions, but when he asked her age she paused and smiled. I found that we were both smiling with her, as if we realised the conventional embarrassment of a woman revealing her age. Eventually she said 'twenty-

one,' which we knew to be correct (in fact she was twenty-two). O'Neil asked her to step on to the scales. 'Schnell!' she said - the German for quick."

During Pierrepoint's brutal and murderous career, he managed to execute up to six hundred men and women, many of which (perhaps like Grese) were innocent of their alleged crimes; Pierrepoint knew some were blameless (from the press controversy and posthumous pardons) but took no action to prevent their deaths, didn't question verdicts instead preferring the malicious excitement he experienced when conducting his macabre task. Whether or not we believe in an eye-for-an-eye, tooth-for-a-tooth coup-de-grace scenario, what kind of beast can put to death those who might be innocent, where he or she might suspect a hint of doubt to their guilt? We are all innocent until proven guilty and that culpability should be thoroughly verified and investigated especially where the threat of a death-sentence is available. It is probable that Irma Grese was only guilty of witness hearsay and idle gossip especially that which flooded British newspapers concerning her case in the wake of her arrest, press reports which must have swayed those gullible jurors.

Making a clear, direct and premeditated decision to end someone's life is no accident so tantamount to murder. Therefore, Pierrepoint was no better than those he hung and just as brutal as an SS thug; the fiend of the court judgement process like that gargoyle who sneers down on us from the precipice of a cathedral wall.

I have written this little story not because of any sympathy with fascist tendencies (in fact I despise Nazis, past and present) but merely because I cannot equate with unfairness, non-impartiality, black lies or injustice. Irma Grese was a young, beautiful woman with her whole life ahead to look forward to; relationships, marriage, a stable home, children and grandchildren. This right to life was cruelly taken from her by a court system which was crudely tacked together by the ifs-and-buts of rumours and many unchallenged lies. Important defence evidence (such as that which could be given by Alice Tenenbaum and others) was not collected or made available. This is another failure and incompetence by the court procedure, actualities which might have saved Irma's life.

Here is another example of Grese's clemency as told by Tommy Schnurmacher in The Canadian Jewish News.

At roll call one morning, mom was singled out by Irma Grese, dubbed the Beautiful Beast of Auschwitz.

Grese "How does a Jew manage to look so clean?"

My mother stared right at her. "I did not like what I was given. I sewed my dress so that it should fit properly. I think it is more important to have shiny shoes than to drink coffee."

The other women figured she was a goner.

Grese was silent for a moment. She could have shot mom right there on the spot. "You are clean enough to work for me. Get back in line, Jew. Starting tomorrow morning, you will report to my living quarters. You will polish my boots. You will tend to my garden. You will be my personal maidservant."

And that is how Irma Grese became the second Nazi to save mom's life.

"She appointed me as her skivvy, or flunky, and that is how I survived."

As a child I recall my mother often telling me that Grese was evil but beautiful; she was blonde and looked like Ingrid Bergman. I was always fascinated to hear the story. I could never hear enough about Irma Grese and always wanted to know more. Throughout my teens and even well into adulthood, I kept peppering my mother with questions about her. In my mind she seemed like a glamorous villain. I always pictured her as a Cat woman-type figure, clad in black leather and wielding a whip.

"Wow, mom! You worked for such a famous evil Nazi. What did she talk to you about?"

"She asked me about my relatives and their ages. She told me my parents had been killed but my brothers and sisters may still be alive. She even managed to find out that my sister Evi was working in the Canada section of the camp sorting the property that had been looted by the Nazis."

"Did you ever see your sister while you were there?"

"Yes. She arranged it. Grese took me to see her and told me we could speak for 10 minutes and no more."

In light of the comments by Schnurmacher as above we should ask ourselves this - are these the acts (or the characteristic nature) of a mass murderer as alleged and condemned? Is it possible that someone showing a degree of compassion and understanding under such austere conditions within a strictly regulated autonomy (where she probably risked her own neck for the good of another) could possibly be a deviant killer? – it would seem highly unlikely.

The 1947 documentary film "The Last Stage" was directed by a Polish woman called Wanda Jakubowska who'd been incarcerated at Auschwitz from April 1943 (just a month after Irma had been posted there) and was later evacuated to Ravensbruck along with Irma Grese. Wanda was imprisoned for being a communist activist; the film's screenwriter and many of the cast had also been imprisoned with her and survived Auschwitz, many of whom were Jewish. The material for the script was drawn from Jakubowska's own experiences and from interviews with other survivors. Irma's character was played by a beautiful Polish actress named Aleksandra Slaska; yet, other than one scene where Irma whips a woman across the breast, none of the cruelty alleged in the Bergen-Belsen court hearing about her is depicted in this film, again indicating Irma's innocence to the charges made against her and to the death penalty imposed.

Irma Grese was stolen from life and from those mind salving moments of a woman's glory, those sweet nuances of womanhood and from the pleasures of being a wife and mother. The thief was Pierrepoint enveloped by a farce of British justice. May God pardon those few indiscretions and rest her troubled soul.

"It's hard to shake hands with liberty when her hands are splattered with blood." Adapted from a quote by Oscar Wilde.

"For the person who tortured me in jail. For the person who tortured the many of my followers and killed them in jail, and the many other greater leaders than me and their followers in jail, and for the men who jailed my supporters, I pray. I don't hate them. I love them as much as I love my closest loved ones, and I pray for their guidance. My loves, you be this way too. It doesn't help to hate. If you hate, you pollute your own soul ... Words cannot express how much I wish the best for you. My foremost ambition for you is that you have hearts full of light, thoughtfulness of God, and goodness, so much so that the devil has no space to get into your hearts. I want you to be happy with yourselves, and for other people to be happy with you, when you leave this life ... May you be so good that rain of mercy falls onto you. May this brother (Ahmad), that is so unworthy of your love, also be so lucky."- Ahmad Moftizadeh

Printed in Great Britain
by Amazon